CW01003497

THE SHOULDER OF SHASTA

THE DESERT ISLAND DRACULA LIBRARY
*promotes the study of Dracula, vampirism,
and the works of Bram Stoker*

THE SHOULDER OF SHASTA
Bram Stoker – Annotated by Alan Johnson 1-874287-30-9

SNOWBOUND: THE RECORD OF A THEATRICAL TOURING PARTY
Bram Stoker – Annotated by Bruce Wightman 1-874287-29-5

THE PRIMROSE PATH
Bram Stoker – Introduced by Richard Dalby 1-874287-21-X

DRACULA: SENSE & NONSENSE
Elizabeth Miller 1-874287-24-4

DRACULA: THE SHADE AND THE SHADOW
Edited by Elizabeth Miller 1-874287-10-4

DRACULA UNEARTHED
Annotated by Clive Leatherdale 1-874287-12-0

DRACULA: THE NOVEL AND THE LEGEND —
A STUDY OF BRAM STOKER'S GOTHIC MASTERPIECE
Clive Leatherdale 1-874287-04-X

THE ORIGINS OF DRACULA — THE BACKGROUND
TO BRAM STOKER'S GOTHIC MASTERPIECE
Clive Leatherdale 1-874287-07-4

TREATISE ON VAMPIRES AND REVENANTS — THE PHANTOM WORLD
Dissertation on those Persons who Return to Earth Bodily, the
Excommuncated, the Oupires or Vampires, Vroucolacas, &c
Dom Augustine Calmet 1-874287-06-6

THE JEWEL OF SEVEN STARS
Bram Stoker – Annotated by Clive Leatherdale 1-874287-08-2

THE LADY OF THE SHROUD
Bram Stoker – Annotated by William Hughes 1-874287-22-8

A GLIMPSE OF AMERICA: AND OTHER LECTURES, INTERVIEWS & FEATURES
Introduced by Richard Dalby 1-874287-35-X

THE SHOULDER
OF SHASTA

by
BRAM STOKER

INTRODUCED AND ANNOTATED BY
ALAN JOHNSON

Series Editor: Clive Leatherdale

Desert Island Books Limited

First Published in United Kingdom in 1895
This annotated edition published in 2000

DESERT ISLAND BOOKS LIMITED
89 Park Street, Westcliff-on-Sea, Essex SS0 7PD
United Kingdom
www.desertislandbooks.com

British Library Cataloguing-in-Publication Data
A catalogue record for this book is available from
the British Library

ISBN   1-874287-30-9

Printed in Great Britain
by
Redwood Books, Trowbridge, Wiltshire

CONTENTS

BIBLIOGRAPHICAL NOTE

The northern California setting of Mount Shasta and San Francisco provides the backdrop of Bram Stoker's only American novel – and yet it has never been published in that country.

It was published in London by Archibald Constable & Co in October 1895, less than two years before they issued his next novel *Dracula*. Although it was strongly produced in a handsome red buckram binding (unlike the shoddily-bound *Dracula*) lettered in gilt with an apple-shaped design surrounding the title in gilt, this book was priced at only three shillings and sixpence (17½ pence) rather than the standard price of six shillings (30 pence).

There was also a simultaneous 'edition intended for circulation only in India and the British Colonies', being No 230 in Macmillan's Colonial Library, with the rear catalogue dated 20 July 1895, and issued in their standard dark green cloth, lettered on the spine in gilt. The title-page stated 'London, Macmillan and Co, and New York, 1895' which was a double contradiction, as no Colonial Edition could legally be sold in either London or New York!

The typesetting of both editions was absolutely identical, with the printer's colophon ('Chiswick Press:– Charles Whittingham and Co., Tooks Court, Chancery Lane, London') appearing on the verso of the final page of text [p.235] in each case. It can be assumed that the same plates were used almost simultaneously by Constable and Macmillan.

The Shoulder of Shasta would probably have been quite popular with American readers, if only they had known about it, especially the suspenseful sequences including the one introduced by Coleridge's famous line from *The Rime of the Ancient Mariner*: '... Because he knows some frightful fiend doth close behind him tread.' Not a supernatural fiend here, merely a great grizzly she-bear ...

Bram Stoker's dedicatee, his elder brother William Thornley Stoker (1845-1912), had just received his knighthood this same year (on the same day as Henry Irving).

Richard Dalby

INTRODUCTION

The first chapter of *The Shoulder of Shasta* describes a rail journey from San Francisco up the Sacramento River valley into northern California: 'As the train ... wound its way by the brawling river, its windows [were] brushed by the branches of hazel and mountain-ash,' and soon 'the road took its serpentine course up and above its own track, over and over again' as the train climbed northward along the twisting banks of the river. Finally, after 'winding up through clearings,' the train arrives at a station, Edgewood, at an elevation of about three thousand feet. Rising another eleven thousand feet in the distance is 'the mighty splendour of Shasta Mountain, its snow-covered head standing clear and stark into the sapphire sky, with its foothills a mass of billowy green and its giant shoulders seemingly close at hand when looked at alone, but of infinite distance when compared with the foreground, or the snowy summit.'

Various details in the novel reveal that the journey takes place at the beginning of a summer in the early 1890s. The railroad itself – the 'Shasta Route,' as it was called – was completed in 1887, for example; and the novel mentions as friends of the central Elstree family – who are English and formerly lived in London – two European musicians who performed in London only after 1890. Photographs from the 1890s or shortly thereafter reveal that the scenic railroad journey was just as Bram Stoker describes it in *The Shoulder of Shasta*.

In fact, on September 17, 1893, Stoker made the same trip. He had travelled to San Francisco in his capacity of business manager for the then-famous Shakespearean actor Henry Irving and his Lyceum Theatre Company of London. Stoker arranged for trans-portation, paid the bills, paid out the salaries, kept the accounts, and was well known to London's theatre-going public as the large, bearded man who supervised the reception of ticket holders at each performance and met many of them individually with a hearty greeting. In the summer of 1893 Irving and his leading lady, Ellen Terry – along with her daughter and the stage-manager, H J Loveday, and his wife – had taken a leisurely trip through Canada and arrived in San Francisco on August 29. Stoker and the rest of the company – about ninety actors and stage technicians – sailed from Southampton on August 19, arrived in New York City, and left immediately for San Francisco in a special train with six cars full of scenery, three sleeping cars, and a 'day' car, according to the San Francisco *Chronicle*, which reported every day of the company's visit to the city with avid interest.[1] After a five-day journey across the United States, Stoker and his group joined the Irving party in San Francisco on Sunday, September 3. Together they began a theatrical tour that would take them north to Seattle, Washington, east to Minneapolis and St Paul, Minnesota, and then to the major cities of eastern United States and Canada.

The company performed in San Francisco at its Grand Opera House for two weeks. The first night, Monday, September 4, was a huge success: 'The vast audience which crowded the great building was beside itself. Men cheered and women clapped' in a show of appreciation such as had been 'never before enacted in any theatre in this city,' according to the *Chronicle*. On Sunday, September 10, the *Chronicle* praised the first week's performances as 'the latest and highest standard of dramatic art,' and that evening the city's prestigious Bohemian Club initiated Irving into their membership at a grand dinner. Stoker, Loveday, and the Lyceum Company's treasurer accompanied Irving. When the members toasted Miss Ellen Terry (who was not present), 'Mr Stoker of the Irving company had the pleasure of responding' with a well-received speech. After the performance on the following Thursday night, Irving entertained members of the club with a splendid supper. He sat at the centre of one side of the long dining table with M H de

---

[1]   See the San Francisco *Chronicle*, August 29 – September 17, 1893, and also Austin Brereton, *The Life of Henry Irving* 2 vols (1908; rpt London: Benjamin Blom, 1969), vol 2, pp186-88.

Young, the editor of the *Chronicle*, on his left and the visiting
Russian Prince Galitzin on his right, while Stoker and Loveday sat
at either end of the table. On Saturday, September 16, the company
concluded its run with 'The Merchant of Venice' for the matinee
and the historical drama 'Louis XI' in the evening. They had played
consistently to capacity audiences, received enthusiastic reviews,
and taken in a gross income of nearly $60,000 – a huge sum for the
period. After the final performance Irving, Ellen Terry, her
daughter, and Stoker joined a certain Ugo Talbo and a few San
Franciscans at a cafe for a supper in honour of Irving's cousin, Mrs
Fred Hubbard, until, according to a reporter who interviewed
Irving after the meal, 'Bram Stoker, the manager of the company,
interrupted the interview to tell Mr Irving that the time was short,
and that they had but a few minutes to catch the boat which left at
1 o'clock' – 1:00am Sunday morning. Irving and his party then
joined the rest of the Lyceum Company members at the Market
Street pier, took a chartered ferry across the San Francisco Bay to
the railhead at Oakland, and departed in the special train for
Portland, Oregon, some five hundred miles to the north, where
they would arrive on Monday morning and offer performances on
the following Tuesday and Wednesday. The journey would take
Stoker past Mount Shasta in the middle of the afternoon of
Sunday, September 17.

In Stoker's often very autobiographical *Reminiscences of Henry
Irving*, he says simply of his Californian experience, 'From San
Francisco we went to Tacoma and Seattle.'[2] Undoubtedly, though,
Stoker's own first biographer Harry Ludlam is exactly right in
saying that 'just a sight, in northern California, of the massive snow-
capped peak of Mount Shasta, the solitary cone of an extinct
volcano, rising splendidly and starkly to the clear blue sky from
foothills a mass of billowy green' was the inspiration for the novel.
Although no manuscript or diary by Stoker seems to survive to
prove the point, Ludlam is very probably correct, too, in saying,
'Before the tour was over he had jotted down another story idea.'[3]

---

[2]   *Personal Reminiscences of Henry Irving*, 2 vols (New York and London: Macmillan,
1906), vol 1, p345.
[3]   Harry Ludlam, *A Biography of Bram Stoker: Creator of Dracula* (London: New

It is quite likely that Stoker wrote as he travelled from city to city across the American continent, but, as he seems to have begun another short novel, *The Watter's Mou'*, in early August, inspired by his holiday visit at that time to Cruden Bay in Scotland, most of his writing of *The Shoulder of Shasta* was probably done after *The Watter's Mou'* was ready for publication in late 1894. *The Shoulder of Shasta* followed from Archibald Constable and Company, Westmin-ster, in October 1895.

~ ~ ~ ~ ~ ~

The Shoulder of Shasta is essentially a romance. The novel has a purportedly realistic Californian setting, considerable – although sometimes ridiculous – humour, an exciting interlude of high adventure, and a rather close, careful study of the developing thoughts and feelings of the heroine, Esse Elstree. It was published by Constable as light reading, and it remains light reading; nevertheless it offers some marvellous natural description and an entertaining, insightful story, and in the final analysis it is an intriguing and informative resource for readers who aim to understand Bram Stoker and his acknowledged masterpiece, *Dracula*, which he had outlined as early as 1890 and published in 1897.

Stoker's creation of a realistic setting for *The Shoulder of Shasta* begins with the Shasta landscape. In all probability he did not enter the Shasta forest himself since he must have been constantly occupied in San Francisco and since the Lyceum Company had less than a day and a half on September 17-18 for its long rail journey past Shasta to Portland. If the train stopped – at Edgewood, for example – it must have moved on quickly. However, Stoker's descriptions of the forest country are vivid – especially those told from the viewpoint of Esse as she travels up to the shoulder of Shasta to the rustic cottage that will be her summer home and as she investigates its surroundings and experiences the fall of evening and the dawn of morning. Stoker conveys both a graphic picture of

English Library, 1977), p101, first published as *A Biography of Dracula – The Life Story of Bram Stoker* (London: W Foulsham and Co), 1962.

the scene and a personal sense of its vastness, vitality, light, darkness, sound, and silence.

Both the wild natural landscape of Mount Shasta and the cityscape of San Francisco are given geographical reality by Stoker's strategic use of place names. It is just possible that the Pacific Ocean could be seen to the west of Mount Shasta, but not very likely, as the novel claims, that the Rocky Mountains could be seen to the east, since Mount Shasta is at the north end of California's Sierra Nevada range and the Rockies lie to the east about five hundred miles across what is known as the Great Basin, which is occupied by the states of Nevada, Utah, and southwestern Idaho. However, Mount Shasta, Edgewood, and the novel's Siskiyou country near them existed and still may be visited by train on the Shasta Route. In San Francisco the Cliff House and Sutro Heights were and are part of the pleasures of the city, although the Cliff House of the novel's era burned down in 1894 and has been rebuilt at least twice since then. Esse's San Francisco home, 'the big house with stone seals on the steps' at 437 California Street may well have corresponded to an actual residence, although now a century of progress has covered the area with corporate skyscrapers.

In clothing and constructing a demeanour for the novel's frontier hero, Grizzly Dick, one suspects that Stoker was in the same position he ascribes to another character, Peter Blyth: 'Like a good many Londoners, his sole knowledge of the actuality of Western life was from "Buffalo Bill" and the "Wild West Show".' Stoker had himself met the great frontier scout, buffalo hunter, and entertainer and almost certainly had attended his Wild West Show in 1887 and 1892 (see Ch 7, note 4). Dick wears buckskins and Mexican spurs, carries a bowie knife, a Winchester rifle, and two revolvers, has a loud, cheery, open manner, and talks in a language peppered with Americanisms and local, Western references. Although the combination of clothing, weapons, and mannerisms nearly amounts to caricature, it encloses a sincere, thoughtful, as well as brave character, and so can seem appropriate to the purposes of the romance.

The one glaring lapse in the novel's verisimilitude is its representation of the Indians of the Shasta area. They are mere stereotypes who serve as helpers, as bystanders, and sometimes as a vehicle for

comic relief. They are presented as Shoshones. The historical
Shoshones, however, did not live in northern California but
eastward, beyond the Sierra Nevada mountains – mainly in
Wyoming and southern Idaho but also in scattered settlements in
the vast area between the Sierra Nevada and Rocky Mountain
ranges. An explanation for this error may lie in an undated nine-
teenth-century magazine illustration reprinted by Lucius Beebe and
Charles Clegg in *San Francisco's Golden Era* (1960). The drawing
shows three Shoshone Indians begging from two well dressed
travellers on a railway platform during a train-stop in Carlin,
Nevada, on the transcontinental route of the Union Pacific and
Central Pacific railroads from the eastern United States to San
Francisco. It is quite possible that Stoker's only direct contact with
Western American Indians was just such an encounter while he and
the Lyceum Company troupe travelled across the United States.
The San Francisco *Chronicle* of September 4, 1893, notes that the
group took the Nevada route westward to California.

In general the setting of the novel presents the familiar contrast
of country and city, 'nature' and 'culture.' The area of 'culture'
extends to England, since many of the characters are English, and it
even extends to Europe since one of them relates in the final
chapter that he has once hunted boar with an emperor – perhaps
Kaiser William II – in a forest in Thuringia. In California, then,
English and European 'culture,' particularly in the person of Esse,
meets American 'nature' and works out an alliance with it. The
story of the meeting, the dilemma of Esse's conflicting attractions,
and the resolution of the dilemma is of course the romance plot.
This plot brings Esse and Dick into close friendship in episodes of
humour and high adventure but depends initially, persistently, and
fundamentally on psychological commentary about Esse's thoughts
and feelings by Stoker as narrator to trace the progress of her two
loves.

~ ~ ~ ~ ~ ~

The humorous episode which helps to bring Esse and Dick together
turns on sheer farce and may strain the modern reader's sensitivities
and sense of what is probable in a purportedly realistic romance. It
turns on old Miss Gimp's unlikely infatuation with Dick and on a

half-witted Indian who supposes, along with other Indians, that, because she possesses an exotic parrot which says 'How,' she is a powerful medicine woman. The humour is simply a play on the reductive stereotypes of the old maid and the Indian. This sort of humour recurs, but the episode also contains a more redeeming and relevant humour, which also recurs – Esse laughs over Miss Gimp, but discovers her own infatuation with Dick.

The adventure which cements the bond between Esse and Dick is pure, high-minded, physical derring-do. Each character is selflessly heroic. Esse, who has been sketching in the woods far from her Shasta cottage, is saved by Dick from almost certain attack by a mother bear; then, with Dick wounded and pinned beneath the bear he has just killed, Esse saves herself and Dick by shooting the dead bear's enraged mate and then carries the injured Dick back to the cottage. Each challenging situation and the action consequent upon it is described in exact and vivid terms. If the farcical humour in the episode of Miss Gimp and the Indian reminds the reader of such humour in Stoker's *Dracula* as Dr Van Helsing's jokes in Chapters 10 and 13 about not giving the 'last drop' of blood in a transfusion and about Lucy Westenra as a 'polyandrist' because she has received transfusions from several men, then perhaps Stoker's meticulous attention to the mechanics of the attacks and rescues in *The Shoulder of Shasta* – to the positions of arms and bodies – will recall the same sort of attention to necks, heads, limbs, and bodies in the many attacks and escapes in *Dracula*.

~ ~ ~ ~ ~ ~

The episodes of humour and adventure in *The Shoulder of Shasta* are not mere diversions. They advance the plot and contribute to the suggestion of a theme of high-minded love in the novel. However, the main focus and source of action in the romance plot is the ongoing process of Esse's thought and feeling, chiefly as the process is revealed by Stoker as the all-knowing narrator of the novel. An important, large, and somewhat difficult example of his psychological analysis occurs early on. The Elstree party has travelled halfway up to the shoulder of Shasta and is camped for the night. Esse stands apart from the camp fire and begins to hear 'the myriad and mystic sounds of the night' – creaking branches, rustling leaves, the fall of water – 'and so, little by little, the life of the night became manifest.' In the morning she witnesses the dawn in a 'mood of semi-religious, semi-emotional exaltation.' The narrator attributes her mood partly to her having read the pantheistic philosophy of Emanuel Swedenborg and poetry of the English 'Lake Poets' (Wordsworth, Coleridge, and Southey), but 'at the present,' the narrator says, her experience of the Shasta wilderness 'proved to her that the Children of Adam' – like herself – 'can only find happiness in concrete reality'; she yearns for some 'incarnation' of the wilderness. Meanwhile 'deep, underlying, unconscious forces of her being were making for some tangible result which would complete her life'; sensing that she is part of 'the whole scheme of Nature' and has some 'destined end' or 'natural purpose' as yet unknown to her, she decides – if that is not too strong a word – that 'she would ... let her feet lead her where instinct took them.' The narrator's description of her thinking is neither simple nor cursory, as it sketches the interplay within her of the stirring of sexual desire, and her acceptance of it, and her conscious urge both to deify the vitality in external nature and to make the deity concrete and personal. Only later, when she listens to Miss Gimp confide her belief that Dick is her secret admirer, does Esse realize that he is the incarnation she has been seeking.

Other passages of psychological analysis up to the final scenes of the novel sustain Esse's thoughts and feelings as the centre and driving force of the romance. Most notably, for example, after the comic episode of Miss Gimp and the Indian, Dick's friendly censure of one of Esse's trivial, life-long mannerisms moves her to attempt to correct it and instils in her, the narrator says, 'that consciousness of effort which marks the border between girl and woman.' At the same time, her new regard for Dick as a mentor 'blinded her to a thousand little roughnesses and coarsenesses' in his behaviour. After the episode of the bears, her idealization of Dick becomes a recurrent object of comment for the narrator. Another particularly notable passage is the narrator's explanation for Esse's shifting feelings once she is back in San Francisco. Her confession to a family friend gives her relief, the narrator says, from 'the strain of self-imposed secrecy,' and the relief frees her to consider a new love.

From this point in the novel onwards the narrator gives very limited analysis of Esse's thoughts. Her predicament creates an amusing scene, but some readers may wish that the narrator had inquired into the thoughts and feelings that would give greater psychological particularity to his comment at this point that her 'romantic feeling for Dick belonged to the school-girl phase of her existence; but the new affection was the expression of her woman's life, and it differed as much from the former in its strength as in its concreteness ... the later and truer love had all the unconscious, serious earnestness of the race itself, where the means are forgotten and only the end is held in view.'

Earlier in the novel the narrator had described Esse not only romanticizing Dick as an incarnation of the wilderness but also discovering an 'instinct' within herself, presumably sexual, that she would trust to lead her to her 'destined end' or 'natural purpose' in 'the whole scheme of Nature.' And later the narrator noted her 'consciousness of effort' in trying to follow Dick's guidance as a sign of her passage 'between girl and woman.' In her relationship with Reginald, an English painter, her sexual attraction to him is clearly implied: he is a handsome fellow; they kiss; and apparently her aim is procreation since she loves with 'all the ... earnestness of the race itself,' the 'end' of which would seem to be perpetuation of the race. Reginald is clearly an able companion and protector for Esse. He has, it seems, saved the life of the European emperor with whom he hunted boar. Reginald's physical abilities make him, like Dick, a 'natural' man, but he is also a man of high culture, at ease in the parlours of San Francisco and at the highest echelons of Euro-pean society. However, because of the abstractness of the narrator's description of Esse's new love as 'the expression of her woman's life,' a reader may easily suppose that this new love for Reginald depends solely on his ability to provide her with the cultivated entertainments and society that she rediscovered with great delight upon her return to San Francisco: shops, music, concerts, visits, dances – 'all those delightful results of civilization.'

How Esse resolves her dilemma can be found in the novel's final chapter. Here she reaches maturity in love and achieves a mediation between the country and the city; nature and culture; new, brash, heroic America and traditional, sophisticated, reliable England. The narrator may have left the last twist of Esse's psychology somewhat unexamined, but clearly culture turns out to include nature in the persons of Reginald and Esse, and mature love chooses culture and keeps in touch with wild, uncultured nature, too.

~ ~ ~ ~ ~ ~

Following publication of *The Shoulder of Shasta* in Britain in late 1895, it received at least a baker's dozen of notices and reviews. Nearly all of them had high praise for its descriptions of natural scenery. Of three reviews in distinctly literary journals, two perceived the novel's general romance plot and gave it high praise. In a brief notice the *Academy* of December 28, 1895, described Esse as 'a young lady of highly impressionable temperament [who] persuades herself that she is enamoured of a stalwart mountaineer ... of the Buffalo Bill type,' and the journal found 'the process by which she becomes disillusioned' to have been 'told with a good deal of humour.' The *Spectator* of February 22, 1896, in a fuller, five-hundred-word review, noted Stoker's analysis of Esse's readiness for love early in the novel and judged that the novel's depiction of the 'rise, progress, and fall' of her 'infatuation' for Dick make 'one fancy that Mr Stoker must have bestowed especial study on girls of Esse's hysterical, emotional temperament.' The *Athenaeum* of November 16, 1895, dismissed the novel in little more than a hundred words and with no specific account of its plot or characters: 'The book bears the stamp of being roughly and carelessly put together. Mr Stoker can probably do much better than this, so perhaps the less said about "The Shoulder of Shasta" the better for everyone concerned.' Nevertheless, those reviewers who gave a fairly close account of the book were charmed by its descriptions and amused by its tale of the rise and fall of a harmless infatuation.

At the opening of the twenty-first century *The Shoulder of Shasta* cannot be read without reference to Stoker's masterpiece, *Dracula*, and the mind that produced it. Very little attention has been paid to *The Shoulder of Shasta* in the more than one hundred years since its first reception. Probably the most incisive and fullest commentary on the novel is Carol Senf's two-page discussion in the Introduction to her book, *The Critical Response to Bram Stoker*.[4] Senf notes the novel's whole romantic triangle (including Reginald), the novel's humour, Stoker's contrast of San Francisco and Shasta, and his praise of 'Anglo-American culture.' She notes, too, that the novel 'celebrates the superiority of civilization over primitive cultures.' The point is painfully accurate although it is notable that when Esse contemplates the primitivity of the Indians she grants that they might make progress, albeit slowly, toward 'higher civilization.' Senf also points out the similarity of Grizzly Dick to *Dracula*'s American, Quincey Morris, and she sees a resemblance between Esse and *Dracula*'s Lucy Westenra 'in her lack of maturity and her as-yet-unawakened eroticism.' If one amends 'as-yet-unawakened' to 'awakening,' the observation becomes provocative, although Esse is diverted by her romantic idealizing of Dick whereas Lucy seems to be diverted by a dissatisfaction – apparently sexual and certainly self-regarding – which is expressed in her whimsical wish that she could marry all three of her suitors.

The Shoulder of Shasta is also notable at the turn of the twenty-first century for its sense of landscape as a window into a 'whole scheme of Nature,' for its apparent assumption of a 'natural purpose,' and for the concept of internationalism with which the novel closes. The novel's sense of a 'whole scheme of Nature' behind visible landscape – 'the Great Scheme,' as Esse calls it in her thoughts – has its root in Stoker's early childhood experience and is, it seems, the basis of the sexual morality (and perhaps the whole morality) in *The Shoulder of Shasta* and arguably in Dracula as well. A clue to Stoker's own affirmation of Esse's notion of 'the Great Scheme' is provided in his comment as narrator as she listens to the sounds of nightfall and discovers 'the life of the night': 'The experience went into Esse's mind, as it must ever go into the mind of man or woman when once it is realized.' Stoker describes his own similar experience in an unpublished passage of his manuscript of *The Personal Reminiscences of Henry Irving*.[5] In the text preceding

---

4   Westport CT and London: Greenwood Press, 1993, pp8-10.

5   See volume 1, pp31-32 of the manuscript, which is at the Folger Shakespeare Library, Washington, DC, and is quoted with the kind permission of the Library and Mr Noel Dobbs. The published context of the passage is in *Personal Reminiscences of Henry Irving*, vol 1, p31.

this passage Stoker makes the point that although he is 'a very
strong man' he had been too weak to stand upright until about the
age of seven. In the unpublished passage he recalls that he was often
'laid down somewhere or other' – sometimes on grass:

> To this day if I lie on the grass those days come back to me
> with never-ending freshness. I look among the stalks or
> blades of the grass & wonder where the sound comes from –
> that gentle hum of nature which never ceases for ears that
> can hear .. [sic] I wonder over what is below the red-brown
> uneven earth which seems so level, but is in reality so rugged.
> Then come back the wisdoms [sic] of those half formed
> thoughts which are the rudiments of philosophy.

This early experience seems to lie behind an incident in the first
chapter of Stoker's novel, *The Snake's Pass* (1890), in which its hero
looks out at the Atlantic Ocean from the head of a deep, rugged
gorge in Galway and is riveted by the scene: 'I wanted to
understand as fully as I could some deep thought which it awoke in
me,' he says, but he can give no explanation of it except that he was
'impressed ... with a sense of the reality of things ... as if ... I passed
into a new and more real life.' In *The Shoulder of Shasta*, however,
the meaning of the landscape is articulated in Esse's thought and is
applied, it seems, by Stoker as the narrator to describe her arrival at
maturity. As she looks at the Shasta scene early in the novel, she
sees the 'Great Scheme' and herself as a part of it; she feels an inner
'instinct'; and she trusts it to lead her to her 'natural purpose.'
When Stoker describes her love for Reginald near the novel's end
as her arrival at 'her woman's life,' he apparently refers to her
fulfillment of her natural purpose in 'the Great Scheme.' The
whole movement of the romance, then, is based in an unusually
explicit way on the value of marriage as a natural purpose of men
and women. Whether it is the sole natural purpose of women, even
women who can defend themselves against wild-animal attacks, the
novel does not say.

The assumption of 'natural purpose' is not made explicit in
Dracula but nevertheless seems to provide both a goal for its romance
plot and the fundamental means by which the characters are

distinguished one from another. Although the pursuit of Dracula takes up much of the novel's action, the ultimate goal of the plot from its outset is the achievement of a productive union for Mina and Jonathan and for Lucy and someone. Dracula, who blocks the way to these unions by captivating Lucy and nearly taking complete control of Mina, is defined as the novel's arch-villain fundamentally by the antithesis of his vampiristic desire to what Stoker sees in the earlier novel as 'natural purpose' in 'the Great Scheme.' Lucy falls victim to the consequences of the desire she expresses with her wish to marry three men at once, while Mina and Jonathan preserve their fidelity to one another, marry, and produce a child. While Stoker retains the notion of 'natural purpose' in *Dracula*, he advances from *The Shoulder of Shasta* by providing an answer (perhaps not a satisfactory one) to the question of whether women's natural purpose is solely marriage. Mina's intellectual, managerial, and psychic abilities are crucial to the collective effort to defeat Dracula, and her resentment at being removed temporarily to protective exclusion by the men is made very clear.

The concept of internationalism, a harmony between nations, is suggested at the end of *The Shoulder of Shasta* by the harmony achieved by Reginald, Esse, and Dick. Like the idea of a scheme of nature, the concept of internationalism has a root in Stoker's own past experience and, as it is dramatized in *The Shoulder of Shasta*, it sheds interesting light on the ending of *Dracula*, with its final tableau of the Dutch Dr Van Helsing, the English Seward, Holmwood, and Jonathan and Mina Harker, and their son Quincey, who has been named after the deceased American, Quincey Morris. Stoker advocated what he explicitly called 'internationalism' as early as November 13, 1872, in a speech to the University of Dublin's College Historical Society. The speech was published as a pamphlet with the title, 'Address Delivered in the Dining Hall of Trinity College,' by James Charles and Son, Dublin, in 1872.[6] Stoker notes the rise of Italy, Germany, France, Russia, the Slavic nations, and the United States as great and ambitious

---

[6]   For permission to make scholarly use of one of the very few surviving original copies of the pamphlet, I am indebted to the late Ann Stoker. It is now in the Trinity College, Dublin, Library. For the material quoted below, see pp18 and 26.

powers and then calls for 'internationalism ... a great idea in the
minds of men, and one which will sway the destinies of the future.'
It is to be a 'casting off of the petty chains of local prejudice ... the
consolidation of all countries into one common league for good....
Internationalism,' he concludes, 'in its true sense, is but the
nationalism of humanity.'

In *Britain's Imperial Century, 1815-1914*, Ronald Hyam explains
that late-nineteenth-century internationalism was in the main a
politically Liberal alternative to an Imperial federation, the device
favoured by Conservatives for governing Britain's widely dispersed
colonies and for preserving Britain's power against other nations.
The Liberal solution to the problem of governing the colonies was
to grant them responsible self-government while retaining them, by
virtue of the good will to be generated by the grant, in a loose union
such as a Commonwealth. According to Hyam, although Liberals
'had no wish to work with colonials, of whom they were frequently
contemptuous,' and although Liberals generally 'liked the empire,'
their 'major loyalty was to the international community' and good
relations with the United States, and 'this loyalty they put before
the empire.'[7] Hyam adds that the idea of Home Rule for Ireland,
which was proposed in Parliament by Prime Minister W E
Gladstone in 1886 and 1893 (and defeated both times) was an
application of the 'internationalism' concept. In *Personal Reminiscences of Henry Irving* (vol 2, p31), Stoker describes himself as
having been 'a philosophical Home-Ruler' during the controversy
over Gladstone's Home Rule bills in the 1880s and early 1890s. The
conclusion of *The Shoulder of Shasta* shows the wide scope of
Stoker's internationalism and its definitely political character by
giving Reginald a friendly relationship with a European emperor as
well as with the American Dick. Stoker shows the British bias of his
internationalism by making Reginald the saviour of the emperor's
life, it seems, during their boar hunt and of course by making
Reginald the suitor who wins Esse. *The Shoulder of Shasta*, with its
concepts of a 'scheme of Nature,' 'natural purpose,' and 'internationalism,' is a piece of light reading which reveals important found-
ations of Stoker's thought and of its expression in *Dracula*.

---

[7]   See Hyam, 2nd ed (Latham MD: Barnes and Noble, 1993), pp250-51.

~ ~ ~ ~ ~ ~

For materials used in the preparation of the Introduction and the notes which accompany the text of the novel, I am indebted to Arizona State University's Hayden and Noble Libraries, the Brotherton Collection at Leeds University, England, the Folger Shakespeare Library in Washington, DC, and the San Francisco Public Library, and to the late Ann Stoker, whose presence is deeply missed by those who knew her. When information in the notes can be found in standard reference works, the source is usually not specified. The *Encyclopaedia Britannica*, 15th edition (1994); the *Oxford English Dictionary on Historical Principles*, 2nd edition (1989); Mitford M Mathews' *Dictionary of Americanisms* (1951); and especially the excellent *New Encyclopedia of the American West*, edited by Howard B Lamar (1998), have consistently been starting places in the search for information. For advice and other support in the preparation of the Introduction and notes, Richard Dalby, Borgny Johnson, and Clive Leatherdale have my sincere thanks. For technical help I am indebted to Mr Glen Trombley and the ASU Humanities Computing Facility.

Alan Johnson
Arizona State University, USA

Publishers' Note:
The text for the current edition has been taken from the Constable original, kindly provided by Richard Dalby. Obvious errors have been corrected, and stylistic changes imposed as follows: quotation marks are single, not double, and full points omitted from initials and abbreviations, for example 'Mr' (not 'Mr.') and G B Shaw (not G. B. Shaw). All page references to *Dracula* are taken from *Dracula Unearthed* (Desert Island Books, 1998).

To
My Brother
SIR THORNLEY STOKER,
President of
The Royal College of Surgeons
In Ireland,
With
Love and Esteem.

ONE

WHEN Mrs Elstree was told that a suitable summer home had been found for her, a certain weight was lifted from her mind. The Doctor whom she had consulted in San Francisco as to her daughter's health was emphatic in his direction that Esse should spend the coming summer high up on some mountain side, and that she should have iron and other natural tonics suitable to her anæmic condition. Dr De Young suggested that on some of the spurs of Shasta, a spot might be found where the air was sufficiently bracing, and where the waters which lower down made the valleys green and bright with their crystal purity had the requisite volcanic qualities. Mrs Elstree had passed by Shasta Mountain[1] once, on her way from British Columbia, and had fallen somewhat under its spell.

It is certainly a wonderful mountain, and has a personality which is rare amongst mountains. The Matterhorn has such a quality, and so have Ranier and Mount Hood;[2] but mountains generally have as little individuality as the items of a dish of peas.

An energetic friend volunteered to make search on Shasta, and after a fortnight's absence telegraphed:

'Have found very spot for you and agreed purchase subject your approval – made deposit; price all told two thousand dollars; strongly advise purchase.' She immediately wired:

---

[1]   Shasta Mountain, usually called Mount Shasta, 14,162 feet high, is located in northern California just to the east of the headwaters of the Sacramento River, which flows south, and about one hundred miles inland from the Pacific coast. Rising eleven thousand feet above the meadows of the river-valley floor, it is visible from a distance of fifty to one hundred miles. The nineteenth-century American naturalist John Muir describes its peak in his *Steep Trails* (1918) as 'the colossal cone of Shasta, clad in ice and snow, ... the pole-star of the landscape.'

[2]   The horn-shaped Matterhorn, 14,962 feet high, is in the Swiss-Italian Alps; 'Ranier,' properly known as Mount Rainier, 14,410 feet, with its huge single-peak glacial system, is fifty miles southeast of Seattle, Washington; and Mount Hood, a snow-covered, symmetrical, extinct volcanic cone 11,245 feet high, is fifty miles east of Portland in northwest Oregon.

'Purchase. Cheque sent payable to you.' The friend was a wise, astute and business-like agent, and when he returned to San Francisco just after an even month's absence he brought with him the deeds of the estate. As to its beauties he would say nothing except an energetic 'Wait. I may be wrong!' When further pressed he added:

'I went there to purchase for you, not myself; but if you don't care about the buy, wire me and I'll take the whole outfit at ten premium!'[3]

The journey from San Francisco seemed to gain new beauty from experience. As the train, after leaving Sacramento,[4] wound its way by the brawling river, its windows brushed by the branches of hazel and mountain-ash, the whole wilderness seemed like the natural pleasaunce of an old-world garden. The road took its serpentine course up and above its own track, over and over again, and the bracing air made the spirits of all the party more eager for a sight of the new summer home. The only exception was Miss Gimp, a good-hearted lady who had been governess of Esse up to the previous year, when she had arrived at her sixteenth birthday, and was now her mother's secretary and companion. Miss Gimp was not altogether satisfied with the whole affair. She had not been consulted about the purchase, she had not even been asked, as an accessory after the fact, if she approved; and worst of all, she had not been there to see that everything was in good order. Mr Le Maistre, who was Mrs Elstree's male factotum,[5] steward, butler, agent, handy-man, engineer and courier, had gone on a week before with the furniture and household effects of all kinds and supplies

---

[3]   A premium, here, appears to be a sum in addition to the purchase price; whether 'ten' refers to a percentage or some other measure of value is not clear.

[4]   The site of Sacramento, on the Sacramento River in central California, fifty miles east of San Francisco, was chosen by J A Sutter for a fort and trading post in 1839. Discovery of gold near his mill in 1848 led to the Gold Rush of 1849. Faced with the influx of prospectors, he helped to establish the city of Sacramento as an extension of the fort in 1848-49. The fort was soon put out of business by the city, which prospered as a centre for food and supplies and later became the state capital in 1854 and the hub city for a railway system, begun in 1862, which eventually extended east across the continent and to the north and south. The northern 'Shasta Route' ran up the Sacramento River valley, over the Siskiyou Pass into Oregon, and on to Seattle, Washington.

[5]   A factotum is a person who 'does all,' a servant who has the entire management of his or her employer's affairs.

wherewith to stock the pantry and wine-cellar. He was to meet them at Edgewood,[6] with horses and ponies, and a suitable guide to bring them to the new house. As he had taken the Saratoga trunks,[7] the present party went flying light as to baggage, and had only to look after their travelling bags and wraps. The live stock was in the special care of Miss Gimp and consisted of a terrier, three Persian cats, and a parrot.

It was but a little after mid-day when the train, winding up through the clearings, drew near the station at Edgewood. The scene was not altogether a promising one. There were too many old meat and vegetable tins scattered about; too many rugged tree-stumps sticking out of the weedy ground, already bare in patches under the heats of the coming summer; insufficient attention to pleasant detail everywhere, and an absolute lack of picturesqueness in the inclined plane formed of rough timber beside the track, and used for purposes of firing and watering the engines. In fact, the whole of the little clearing was in that stage of development when beauty stands equally apart from nature and utility. But there was one sufficient compensation for all the immediate squalor. Beyond, in the distance, rose the mighty splendour of Shasta Mountain, its snow-covered head standing clear and stark into the sapphire sky, with its foothills a mass of billowy green, and its giant shoulders seemingly close at hand when looked at alone, but of infinite distance when compared with the foreground, or the snowy summit.

There is something in great mountains which seems now and then to set at defiance all the laws of perspective. The magnitude of the quantities, the transparency of cloudless skies, the lack of regulating sense of the spectator's eye in dealing with vast dimensions, all tend to make optical science like a child's fancy. Up at the

---

[6]   Edgewood is a small town about fifteen miles northwest of Mt Shasta's summit on the road and railroad from Sacramento to Portland in Oregon, and to Seattle. Established in 1851, it became a popular stopping place after William Cavanaugh opened a hotel there in 1860, according to Phil Townsend Hanna's *Dictionary of California Land Names* (1951).

[7]   The Saratoga trunk, a large trunk, usually with a rounded top, took its name from the fashionable spa-resort town of Saratoga Springs at the foot of the Adirondack Mountains and near the Hudson River in northeastern New York state. The *Oxford English Dictionary* notes that the trunk was 'much used by young ladies.'

present height, nearly three thousand feet, the bracing air began to tell on their spirits. Even Esse's pale cheeks began, to her mother's great delight, to show some colour, and her dark eyes flashed with unwonted animation, as they ranged over the splendid prospect. She rushed up to Le Maistre, who was signalling some men on the far side of the clearing to bring the horses which were tethered in the shelter of the great pine-trees, and exclaimed:

'Where is our place? Point it out to me; I am simply perishing to know all about it!' Le Maistre turned round, and then pointed to the northern shoulder of the mountain.

'There, miss, on the left hand of the mountain, a little way below that sharp curve that looks like an old volcano!' Esse looked, and her heart leaped high. On the northern shoulder of the great mountain lay a little plateau where could be seen in the distance the green undulation of forest with here and there a great conifer towering out of the mass. As it lay to the western side of the moun-tain, it was manifest that it must command the whole range of the seaboard. There was this added charm, that just below it was a thin white line of rushing water, so that there must be some lake or tarn at hand. Mrs Elstree shared in the joy when Esse ran towards her impulsively, calling out:

'Hurry, mother! hurry, or we'll never get there!' It was many a long day since Esse had shown so much interest in anything, and the mother's heart was glad that already the mountain had begun its invigorating work.

It took a little time to get the little caravan in order, and Mrs Elstree utilized the time in making Esse take something to eat. A cup of tea was soon made ready by the obliging wife of the station-master, and some San Franciscan sandwiches formed the rest of the improvised meal. As soon as she could do so without altogether disappointing her mother, Esse hurried out and found Le Maistre, with his companions, ready to set out when the word should be given. Le Maistre was himself somewhat of a picturesque figure, for he was a tall, fine man, with good features, and a black beard tinged with grey; and he was dressed in a suitable compromise between his domestic occupation and the requirements of his new surround-ings. He had riding trousers and high boots, a flannel shirt, and a short cutaway coat;[8] altogether he looked like a Western version of an English squire. But his glories entirely paled before the picturesque appearance of his companions. Some of these were Indians, bronze-coloured, black-haired, high cheek-boned, lithe fellows who made announcement to all men of the fact of their being civilized by the nondescript character of their attire. Some had old red coats of the British infantry,[9] and some the ragged remains of fashionable trousers; but they still wore some of their barbaric feathers, trinkets and necklaces of bone and teeth; and most of them had given themselves a mild coat of paint in honour of the occasion. They were all armed with rifles, and their lassos hung over their arms.

The most picturesque figure of the group by far was, however, a tall, handsome mountaineer who stood leisurely fastening a new whip lash beside a sturdy little Indian pony at the head of the cavalcade. He was dressed in a deerskin shirt marked with the natural variations of the tanning, and stained with weather, and with fringes cut in its own stuff at neck and sleeve. It was beautifully embroidered in front and round the neck with fine Indian work of bead and quill. He wore his fair hair long so that it fell over his shirt collar and right down his back. In his belt of dressed deerskin was a huge bowie knife[10] and two revolvers;[11] buckskin breeches and great

---

[8]   A cutaway coat has its skirt cut back from the waist in a downward curve.

[9]   The possession of British infantry clothing by Shasta-area Indians in the early 1890s, the period in which the story is set, is historically unlikely since the United States had taken California from Mexican control in 1848 and had received sole possession of the Oregon territory (including the present-day states of Oregon, Idaho, and Washington) in 1846. That area had been claimed by the US and Britain following landings by Britain's Captain James Cook in 1778 and the American Captain Robert Gray in 1791; it was used by both nations as 'free and open' from 1825 to 1846, with the British Hudson's Bay Company dominating the area's fur trade in the early years of the period from its main depot at Fort Vancouver on the Columbia River, between the present-day Oregon and Washington, but after 1846 the troops policing the territory were American.

[10] A bowie knife is a sheath knife with a strong single-edged blade about nine to fifteen inches long, often having a sharp or semi-sharp edge on the top of the blade from its point backwards for several inches and a guard between the blade and handle. It takes its name and fame from Colonel James Bowie (1796-1836), a Louisiana planter and slave trader in the 1820s who moved to Texas in 1828, where he tried mining and other ventures and died at the Alamo while fighting with the Texas army in its struggle to win independence for Texas, which was then a part of Mexico. The original knife was made for Bowie by an Arkansas blacksmith (his brother Rezin or more probably one James Black). Its fame spread by oral and newspaper reports, often highly fanciful, of incidents such as Bowie's supposed self-defence against three assassins in 1830 by decapitating the

riding boots, with big Mexican spurs,[12] completed his dress. The
saddle of his mustang was of the heavy cowboy pattern, with flaps to
cover the rider's feet; a Winchester rifle[13] and a curled-up raw-hide
lasso lay across the saddle. There was about him a free and resolute
bearing – the easy natural carriage of one conscious of his power,
and that complete absence of fear, and even of misgiving, which
mark the King of Beasts in his own sphere. Le Maistre called him
up:

'Hi! Dick!' The man turned and came forward with the long,
easy, swaying stride of a mountaineer, and as he came raised his
beaver-skin cap. Le Maistre introduced him:

'This is Dick, Miss Esse. He is a neighbour up at Shasta, and has
kindly undertaken to Mr Hotteridge to look after us all. It's no
mean thing either, Miss, in a place where there are still lots of
grizzlies, and the Indians are – well, you see yourself what they are!
This man they call Grizzly Dick because he's killed so many!' Dick
took the compliment with true Indian stoicism, and simply turned
to Esse and held out a huge brown hand. As she placed her little

---

first, disembowelling the second with an upward lunge from the ground, and splitting
the skull of the third as he fled. Manufacture of the bowie knife flourished in the US and
in such centres as Sheffield in Britain. It saw wide use on the American frontier and
became a popular ceremonial gift throughout the country. See Raymond Thorp, *Bowie
Knife* (1948), William G Keener's catalogue, *Bowie Knives*, for the Ohio State Historical
Society, 1962, and for Bowie himself, William C Davis, *Three Roads to the Alamo* (1998).

[11]   Samuel Colt (1814-1862) produced the first efficient repeating pistol by inventing
the revolving cylinder, bored to accommodate five or six cartridges, patented in the US in
1836. Popular in the Mexican War of 1846-48, the Colt revolver saw widespread use for
the rest of the nineteenth century.

[12]   Mexican spurs have a large rowel for urging the wearer's horse forward and often
bear silver ornamentation.

[13]   The Winchester rifle, manufactured beginning in 1866 by Oliver F Winchester
(1810-1880), was a breech-loading rifle with a tubular magazine under the barrel and a
horizontal bolt operated by a lever (the trigger guard) on the underside of the stock, and
it used newly developed metallic-cartridge ammunition. It could fire sixteen shots in
rapid succession and was a refinement on its predecessor, the 1860 Henry rifle. Prior to
these weapons, rifles had to be reloaded manually after each firing. Of the rugged, .44
calibre, 1873 model Winchester, Colonel W F 'Buffalo Bill' Cody wrote in 1875, 'For
general hunting, or Indian fighting, I pronounce your improved Winchester *the boss.*'
See Harold F Williamson, *Winchester: The Gun That Won the West* (1952). Stoker has
provided Dick with the complete set of nineteenth-century frontier weapons in the bowie
knife, the revolver, and the Winchester. The bowie knife and the Winchester both
feature prominently in *Dracula*.

one in it he wrung it with such strength and exuberant vitality, that she felt almost inclined to cry out as he spoke:

'How d'ye, Little Missy. Glad ter see ye. You'n me'll be pards I guess. When ye want anything, count me in every time!' While he was speaking, Mrs Elstree drew close and held out her hand, saying:

'Glad to see you, Mr Grizzly Dick. I hope you're going to take me on in the little game!'[14] She showed her dazzling white teeth, her blue eyes flooded with merriment, and her tangle of gold hair shook like the fleck of falling sunshine. Dick rubbed his brown palm on the thigh of his buckskin breeches, and then took her hand in his with a grip that made her wince. When she withdrew her cramped fingers, she said:

'By the way, are you Mr Grizzly Dick or Mr Dick Grizzly? If that is your friendly shake, I must look out for a real grizzly when I want a mild one!' Dick threw back his head and laughed with a glee and a resonance which plainly showed that not only his heart, but all his other vital organs were sound. Then Esse and her mother mounted, and Dick, sending two Indians ahead, rode beside them on their way to Shasta.

The sun was hot, and when they rode through clearings between the trees, the air seemed to hold the heat till it quivered from the moist ground to the tree tops high above them; but there was a delicious sweetness and fragrance from the pines, and the rarefied air of the high plateau braced them to the pitch of joyousness. Esse felt that she could never forget that journey; there was such an adventurous, picnicing air about everything, that she was afraid of losing a moment of the time.

For most part of the journey of that day, the snow cap of Shasta was hidden from them by the great trees that seemed to rise all round them; but every now and then, on surmounting a ridge that whilst its ascent was being made seemed itself like a mountain, they caught a glimpse of the noble dome before them rising in silent grandeur. In the early part of the afternoon their path was almost entirely through the forest, where the hoofs of the ponies fell silently on the mass of pine needles. There were myriads of ant-hills,

---

[14]   Mrs Elstree apparently picks up Dick's reference to poker (or any card game), 'Count me in.' Stoker repeats the expression in *Dracula;* see *Dracula Unearthed* p114.

sometimes rising in open spaces of the glade like little brown
mounds of moving items – coherent masses of strenuous endeavour
– or piled against and around the fir-trees, up and down whose
rugged stems the armies of the ants seemed to be ever moving.
More than once they had to make a long and deep descent into a
valley, in order to cross a stream which looked from above like a
silver thread, but which when they reached it had to be forded with
the greatest care. But still the way they were winning was upward,
and each time they emerged from a stretch of forest the air was
appreciably colder, due both to the height they had climbed, and to
the oncoming night.

Towards evening, they picked out a spot for a camp on a little
spur of rocky ground overlooking a deep valley. There were here
only a few tall pines whose bare and rugged appearance bore
witness to their constant exposure. How they ever came to be there
was a wonder to Mrs Elstree, till she saw the spring of sweet water
which bubbled up close to their roots, and trickling away fell over
the precipice into the valley below. The instant the word was given,
the preparation for the bivouac began. Some of the Indians took
from their ponies the material for a little bell-tent, such as soldiers
use, and in what appeared to Esse to be an incredibly short time,
had it fixed, pegged down and banked up with earth from a trench
which they dug round it. At the same time some of the others had
got wood, and lighted a fire over which they had hung the cooking-
pot for their evening's meal. Le Maistre had in the meantime
busied himself with his own preparations for dinner. He had
lighted a small fire in a circle of loose stones, and placed over it
what looked like a square box, which presently began to give out
appetizing odours. A rough table was formed from a log, and
campstools were placed beside it; and before Esse could get over her
wonderment at the whole scene, she found that dinner was ready to
be served. The evening was now close at hand, and the beauty of the
scene arrested the hungry mortals who had the privilege of seeing it.
The sun was sinking like a great red globe into the Pacific, and from
the great height at which they were, the rays reached them from
over a far stretch of the earth below them, now shrouded in the
black shadow of the evening. High above and beyond them, when
they looked back, the rosy light fell on the snowy top of the

mountain, and lit it with a radiance that seemed divine.

And then the sun seemed to pass from them, and they too were hidden in the shadow of the night; but still the light fell on the mountain till the darkness, creeping up, seemed to wipe it out. When the last point of light had faded from the white peak, which the instant after seemed like the ghost of itself, they looked down, and seemed to realize that the night was upon them.

Dinner was waiting them, so as soon as the entire landscape was blotted out, they bethought them of their hunger. By the time they had sat down at the rude table the Indians had lighted some pine branches and stood round holding them as torches.

It was a wonderful sight. The red flare of the burning pine threw up the red trunks of the great pine-trees so that they seemed to tower towards the very skies, until they were lost in distance, and behind them their black shadows seemed to fall into the depths of the valley. Esse felt like some barbaric empress, and could not take her mind off the picturesque and romantic aspect of the whole thing. It seemed a piece of nightmare projection of the present on the past whenever Le Maistre, in the course of the meal, changed his enamelled tin plates, or brought a fresh variety of food from his mysterious box. Mrs Elstree was full of the beauty of the scene; and as she looked at the happiness on her daughter's face, and noted the quick eagerness which had already taken the place of the habitual languor, she felt a great peace stealing over her, much as sleep creeps over a wearied child.

Esse did not stay longer at the table than was necessary. In the thoughtlessness of her youth she overlooked the fact that the others of the party were hungry, and, only for her mother's whispered warning, she would at once have joined the group awaiting round the camp fire the completion of the cookery. The Indians sat on one side of the fire and ate their meat half cooked – part of a little deer which Dick had shot, on purpose for the meal, just before sunset. Le Maistre and Dick sat together at the opposite side of the fire, and took their dinner with the larger deliberation of the Caucasian.[15] Still, there were not many courses to be served, and it

---

[15]   'With the larger deliberation of the Caucasian' is the first of several very explicit instances in the novel of what might be called 'imperialist' anthropological categorization.

was not long till both men had got out their pipes and were beginning to enjoy a smoke. The Indians had already lit their corn-cobb pipes, and were in high enjoyment, squatted down close enough to the fire to have begun the cookery of a white man. When Esse saw the puffs of smoke she at once went over to the fire. Le Maistre jumped to his feet and took his pipe from his mouth; but Dick sat still and smoked on. Esse said, as she came close:

'If you stop smoking I shall go away; and I want to come and ask you things.' Le Maistre at once sat down and resumed his pipe, and Esse sat on a broken trunk and watched the fire. All the while Miss Gimp was sitting with Mrs Elstree, asking questions as to the best way of finishing a new pattern of crochet which had hitherto baffled her. Esse's first question to Dick was:

'Why have we chosen this spot to camp in? Suppose a high wind were to come, wouldn't it blow the tent over the precipice?'

'That's true enough, Little Missy, but there ain't no high wind a-comin' up the cañon to-night – nothin' more than the sea-wind which is keepin' the smoke off this here camp. An' even if it did come, well, we've got fixin's on to these trees that I reckon'll see the night through. As to choosin' this spot, where is there a better? See, we've shelter from the big trees, an' water here to hand, so with a fire across the neck of this rock, and one man to watch it, where's the harm to come from, and how's it goin' to reach us?'

'I see,' said Esse, and was silent for a while, taking in and assimilating her first lesson in woodcraft. After a little bit she strolled away to the northern side of the precipice, and stood at the edge, wrapt in the glorious silence. A little way off the great fire, which the Indians had heaped with branches, leaped and threw lurid lights on its own smoke, which, taken by the west wind, seemed to bend over and disappear into the darkness of the valley like falling water. Overhead was the deep dark blue of the night, spangled with stars that seemed through the clear air as if one had only to stretch out a hand to touch them; and high away to the south rose the snow-cap of Shasta gleaming ghostly white.

After a while the silence itself became oppressive, as though the absence of sound were something positive which could touch the nervous system. Esse listened and listened, straining her ears for any sound, and at length the myriad and mystic sounds of the night began to be revealed; the creaking of branches and the whispering rustle of many leaves; the fall of distant water; and now and then the far away sound of some beast of the night began to come through the silence. And so, little by little, the life of the night, which is as ample and multitudinous as the life of the day, had one but knowledge to recognize its voices, became manifest; and as the experience went into Esse's mind, as it must ever go into the mind of man or woman when it is once realized, the girl to whom the new life was coming felt that she had learned her second lesson in woodcraft.

And so she sat thinking and thinking, weaving from the very fabric of the night such dreams as are ever the elixir of a young maiden's life,[16] till she forgot where she was, and all about the wonders of the day that had passed, and wandered at will through such starlit ways as the future opened for her.

She was recalled to her surroundings by some subtle sense of change around her. The noises of the night and the forest seemed to have ceased. At first she thought that this was because her ears had become accustomed to the sounds; but in a few seconds later she realized the true cause; the moon was rising, and in the growing light the sounds, which up to then had been the only evidence of Nature's might, became at once of merely ordinary importance. And then, all breathless with delight, Esse, from her high coign of vantage on the brow of the great precipice, saw what looked like a ghostly dawn.

Above the tree-tops, which became articulated from the black mass of a distant hill as the light shone through the rugged edge, sailed slowly the great silver moon. With its coming the whole of Nature seemed to become transformed. The dark limit of forest, where hill and valley were lost in mere expanse, became resolved in some uncertain way into its elements. The pale light fell down great slopes, so that the waves of verdure seemed to roll away from the light and left the depths of the valleys wrapped in velvety black. Hill-tops unthought of rose in points of light, and the great ghostly dome of Shasta seemed to gleam out with a new, silent power.

---

[16] Generalizations based on gender such as the one used here recur frequently in the novel with regard to both male and female characters.

Esse had begun to lose herself again in this fresh manifestation
of Nature's beauty when her mother's voice recalled her to herself.
She went over to the tent and found her busily engaged with Miss
Gimp in arranging matters for the night. The tent was so tiny that
there was just room for the three women to lie comfortably on the
piles of buffalo and bear rugs which were laid about; and Esse
having seen her own corner fixed, went out and stood by the fire
where Dick and Le Maistre still sat smoking and talking. She had
taken a bearskin robe with her, and this she spread on the ground,
near enough to hear the men talk, and sat on it, leaning back on
one elbow, and gazed into the fire. She did not feel sleepy; but sleep
had been for many a day an almost unknown luxury. For hours
every night had she lain awake and heard the clocks chime, and
sometimes had seen the dark meet with the dawn, but when sleep
had come, it had come unwillingly, with lagging and uncertain step.
But for very long she had not known that natural, healthy sleep
which comes with silent footstep, and makes no declaration of his
intent. The bright firelight flickered over her face, now and again
making her instinctively draw back her head as a collapsing branch
threw out a fresh access of radiance. And she thought and thought,
and her wishes and imaginings became wrought into her strange
surroundings. All at once she sat up with sudden impulse as she
heard Dick's voice in tones of startling clearness:

'Guess Little Missy's fallen asleep. You'd better tell her mother
to get her off to bed!' With the instinctive obedience of youth and
womanhood to the voice of authority she rose, swaying with sleep,
and saying good-night passed into the tent. Here she found her
mother wrapping herself in her blanket for the night. Esse made
her simple toilet, and in a few minutes she too was wrapped in her
blanket and was settling down to sleep. Then Miss Gimp put out
the dark lantern which was close to her hand, and in a very few
minutes, what she would have denied as being a snore, proclaimed
that she slept. Mrs Elstree was lying still, and breathed with long,
gentle breaths. Esse could not go to sleep at once, but lay awake
listening. She heard some sounds as of men moving, but nothing
definite enough to help her imagination in trying to follow what
was happening outside. She raised herself softly, and unlooping one
of the flaps of the tent looked out.

The fire still blazed but with the strong settled redness, that shows that there is a solid base of glowing embers underneath the flame, and round it were stretched several dark figures wrapped in gaily coloured blankets. In the whole camp was only one figure upright; at the neck of the little rocky promontory stood a tall figure leaning on a Winchester rifle, seeming to keep guard over the camp. He was too far off to be touched by the firelight, but the moonlight fell on the outline of his body and showed the long fair hair falling on the shoulders of his embroidered buckskin shirt. When he turned she could see the keen eagle eyes looking out watchfully.

Esse crept back to her bed, and, with a contented sigh, fell asleep.

TWO

ESSE became awake all at once, and, throwing off the buffalo robe which covered her, opened the flap of the tent and looked out. Over everything was the cold light of the coming dawn. The Indians were moving about and piling up again the fire, which was beginning to answer their attention with spluttering crackles, and Grizzly Dick was blowing a tin mug of steaming coffee which Le Maistre had just handed to him. Esse hurried her toilet in a manner which would have filled Miss Gimp with indignant concern, had she been awake, and stole out of the tent. She went over to the eastern side of the plateau, and stood there, looking expectantly for the coming dawn. It was something of a shock when Dick handed to her a mug of hot coffee saying:

'Catch hold! Guess, Little Missy, ye'd better rastle this or the cold of the morning 'll get ye, sure!' She took the coffee, and, although at first she felt it a sort of sacrilege to superadd the enjoyment of its consumption to the more ethereal pleasure of the sea of beauty around her, was glad a moment later for the physical comfort which it gave her. As she looked, the eastern sky commenced to lose its pallor; and then, softly and swiftly, the whole expanse of the horizon began to glow rosy red. As the light grew, the stretch of forest below began to manifest itself in a sea of billowy green. Wave after wave of forest seemed to fall back into the distance, till far away, beyond a great reach of dimness which seemed swathed in mist, the myriad peaks of the Rocky Mountains began to glow under the coming dawn. And then a great red ray shot upward, as though some veil in the sky had been rent, and the light of the eternal sun streamed through. Esse clasped her hands in ecstasy, and a great silence fell on her. This silence she realized as strange a moment after, for with the first ray of sunlight all the rest of Nature seemed to spring into waking life. Every bird – and the forest seemed to become at once alive with them – seemed to hail the dawn with the solemn earnestness of a Mahomedan at the voice of the muezzin,[1] and the full chorus of Nature proclaimed that the day had come. Esse stood watching and watching, and drinking in consciously and unconsciously all the rare charm and inspiration of Nature, and a thousand things impressed themselves on her mind, which she afterwards realized to the full, though at the moment they were but unconsidered items of a vast mutually-dependent whole. Like many another young girl of restless imagination, at once stimulated and cramped by imperfect health, she had dipped into eccentric forms of religious thought. Swedenborgianism[2] had at one time seemed to her to have an instinctive lesson which was conveyed in some more subtle form than is allowed of by words. Again, that form of thought, or rather of feeling, which has been known as of the 'Lake School,'[3] had made an impression on her, and she had so far accepted Pantheism as a creed that she could not dissociate from the impressions of Nature the idea of universal sentience. What the moral philosophers call 'natural religion,' and whose methods of education are of the emotions, had up to the present satisfied a soul which was as yet content to deal with abstractions. This content is the content of youth, for things concrete demand certain severities of thought and attitude which hardly harmonize with the easy-going receptivities of the young. At the present the whole universe was to Esse a wonderland, and its potentialities of expression and of deep meanings which she yearned for, and she could not realize – and did not in her ignorance think of the subject – proved to her that the Children of

---

[1]   A muezzin in the Muslim religion is a public crier who proclaims the regular hours of prayer from a minaret or the roof of a mosque.

[2]   The Swedish natural scientist, philosopher, and theologian Emanuel Swedenborg (1688-1772) held that the fundamental element of all things in nature, including humans, is material particles in motion, that this motion manifests power and life and is God, and that the natural, material world, except for deviations caused by man's misuse of his free will, corresponds to another, 'spiritual,' world. Followers of his theology founded what they called the New Church in 1788, but Swedenborgianism refers to any advocacy of his theology.

[3]   The 'Lake School' is the name given in their own time, the early nineteenth century, to the poets William Wordsworth, Samuel Taylor Coleridge, and Robert Southey, who all lived in the English Lake District. The first two particularly wrote frequently about natural scenery and suggested the existence of a seemingly, and sometimes explicitly, divine force in the natural world, as Coleridge does in the poem, 'The Eolian Harp' (1795), lines 44-48 of which are quoted in the next paragraph of this chapter.

Adam, being finite in all their relations, can only find happiness in
concrete reality. The religion of the men of Athens who set up their
altars 'To The Unknown God'[4] was a type of the restless spirit of an
unsatisfied longing, and not merely a satisfied worship of something
beyond themselves. Not seldom in Greece of old did youth or
maiden pass weary hours in abasement before a statue of Venus or
Apollo, hoping for the incarnation of the god. So Esse in her
unsatisfied young life watched and waited at the shrine of Nature,
not knowing what she sought or hoped for, whilst all the time the
deep, underlying, unconscious forces of her being were making for
some tangible result which would complete her life.

Now, as she stood alone in the springing dawn, with the entire
world seemingly at her feet, she began to feel that in the whole
scheme of Nature was one deep underlying purpose in which each
thing was merely a factor; that she herself was but a unit with her
own place set, and the narrow circle of her life appointed for her, so
that she might move to the destined end. It might be destiny, it
might be fate, it might be simply the accomplishment of a natural
purpose; but whatever it might be, she would yield herself to the
Great Scheme, and let her feet lead her where instinct took them.
And as she sighed in relief at not having to struggle any more – for
so the emotion took her – she found herself repeating Coleridge's
lines:

'And if that all of animated Nature
Be but organic harps diversely framed,
That tremble into thought as o'er them sweeps
Plastic and vast one intellectual breeze –
At once the soul of each and God of all.'[5]

It was not, she felt, all fancy that the gentle sweet wind of the dawn
took the pine-needles overhead, and rustled them in some sort of

---

[4]   See the Bible, Acts 17.22-23, which describes Paul saying, while in Athens, 'Ye men
of Athens ... as I passed by, and beheld your devotions, I found an altar with this
inscription, "To the Unknown God".' In the polytheistic Athenian religion, the altar was
intended for any gods who might have been excluded in the dedication of altars to
named gods.
[5]   See note 3, above. The first line should begin, 'And what if all.'

divine harmony with the poet's song.

Esse's mood of semi-religious, semi-emotional exaltation was
brought to an end by Dick, who came and stood beside her, and
said, as he pointed with a wide, free sweep of his arm to the whole
eastern panorama:

'Considerable of a purty view, Little Missy!'

'Oh, beautiful, beautiful! How you must love it who live here in
the midst of it all. I suppose you were born on Shasta?' Dick
laughed:

'Guess not much! I was raised somewhere out on the edge of the
Great Desert.[6] Mother couldn't abide mountings, and kept dad
down in the bottoms.'

'Then how did you ever come to Shasta?'

'Wall, dad he lived by huntin' an' trappin' an' when the Union
Pacific came along, he found the place got too crowded; so he made
tracks for Siskiyou![7] But, Lordy! it didn't seem to be no time at all
till the engineers began runnin' new lines between Portland and
Sacramento.[8] So says dad: 'If the Great American Desert ain't good
enough to let a man alone in, an' if he gets crowded out of the
chaparral at Siskiyou, then durn my skin but I'll try the top of the
mountings,' so we up sticks and kem up here!'

'And your mother?' asked Esse, sympathetically; 'how did she

---

[6] 'Great Desert' is a short form of 'Great American Desert,' used two paragraphs later.
The latter term was coined in 1823 by the Rocky Mountain explorer Major Stephen
Long to designate the present-day Great Plains east of the Rockies and the then virtually
unexplored westward area between the Rockies and the Sierra Nevada mountain range.
According to Eugene Hollon's *The Great American Desert* (1966), the term's reference
shrank to the westward area alone by the 1890s.

[7] Construction of the Union Pacific Railroad westward from Omaha, Nebraska, met
Central Pacific Railroad construction eastward from San Francisco at Promontory Point,
Utah, in 1869. In 1880-84 the Union Pacific line was also extended from southwest
Wyoming to the northwest around the northern edge of the Great Desert to Portland,
Oregon. Southern routes to the Pacific coast were built through New Mexico and
Arizona by other companies in the 1880s (see Robert G Athearn's *Union Pacific Country*,
1971, and the *Rand McNally Atlas of American Frontiers*, 1993). Siskiyou designates a
county in northernmost California. Mt Shasta is in the southeast quarter of the county;
the Siskiyou Mountains occupy its northwest sector and extend into southern Oregon.

[8] Construction of the rail connection between Portland and Sacramento – the 'Shasta
Route' – began from each city in 1872; after a ten-year hiatus the northward construction
resumed and passed through Siskiyou County in 1886-87, joining the southward line in
late 1887 at Ashland, Oregon, according to W Harland Boyd's *The Shasta Route* (1981).

bear the change?'

'Lor' bless ye! she didn't hev no change; why before we ever went to Siskiyou, she up an' took a fever, an' died. Me an' dad scooped a hole for the old lady 'way down by One Tree Creek.[9] Dad said as how he didn't see as she'd be able to lie quiet even there, with fellers bringin' along school-houses, an' dancin' saloons, an' waterworks, and sewin' machines, an' plantin' them down right atop of her. Ye see, Little Missy, the old man were that fond of nobody that he didn't take no stock whatever in fash'nable life – like you an' me!' A ghost of a smile flickered at the corners of Esse's mouth; she was not herself in any way addicted to 'society' life, but rather longed for the wilderness – in an abstract form, and of course free from discomforts; but between Dick and herself there was so little in common – that was Dick's very charm – that she wondered what might be the nature of that fashion which took them both within its limits to the exclusion of others. She was, however, interested in the man, and curious as to his surroundings, so she made an interrogative remark:

'Of course you love living on the mountain; and never go into a town at all?'

'Never go into a town! I should smile! Only whenever I can, and then, oh Lordy! but that town comes out all over red spots!' Again Esse made another searching remark:

'I suppose your wife goes with you!' Dick laughed a loud, aggressive, resonant laugh, which seemed to dominate the whole place. The Indians, hearing it, turned to gaze at him, and as Esse looked past his strong face, jolly with masculine humour and exuberant vitality, at their saturnine faces, in which there was no place for, or possibility of a smile, and contrasted his picturesqueness, which was yet without offence to convention, with their unutterably fantastic, barbarous, childish, raggedness, she could not help thinking that the Indian want of humour was alone sufficient to put the race in a low place in the scale of human types. Dick continued to roar. 'My wife,' he said, 'my wife. Ha! ha! ha! Wall,

---

[9]   No One Tree Creek is listed in the US Geological Survey's Geographic Names and Information System for the area probably designated by Dick's 'edge of the Great Desert,' but a Lone Tree Creek exists in that area, east of California's Yosemite Park.

that's the best joke I heard since I see the Two Macs at Virginia City[10] a twelvemonth ago.' Then he became suddenly grave. 'Askin' yer pardon, Little Missy, fur laffin' at yer words, but the joke is, I ain't got no wife. No sir! not much!' Here he turned away to avoid wounding her feelings, and his face was purple with suppressed laughter as he passed beyond the fire, where she heard his laughter burst out afresh amongst the Indians. Esse looked after him with a smile of amused tolerance. With a woman's forbearance for the opposite sex – whether the object deserved it or not does not matter – she felt herself drawn to the man because of her forgiveness of him. The laughter, however, had completely dispersed the last fragments of her pantheistic imaginings, and she realized that the day was well begun; and so she went to the tent to her mother.

When she opened the flap and entered, she felt a sense of something out of harmony. The white walls of the tent were translucent enough to let in sufficient light to show up everything with sufficient harshness to be unpleasant. Mrs Elstree and Miss Gimp still slept; the former lying on her side, with her golden hair in a picturesque tangle, and her bosom softly rising and falling; the latter on her back, with her mouth open, and snoring loudly. Her hair was tightly screwed up over her rather bald forehead, and in her appearance seemed to be concentrated all that was hard in Nature, heightened by the resources of art. Esse bent down and kissed her mother, and shook her gently, telling her that it was time to get up. Then she woke Miss Gimp, with equal gentleness, but with a different result. Mrs Elstree had waked with a smile, and seeing before her her daughter's bright face, had drawn it down and kissed her. Miss Gimp woke with a snort, which reminded Esse of one time when her umbrella stick had snapped in a high wind, and,

---

[10] This might refer to Virginia City in distant Montana but almost certainly refers to Virginia City, Nevada, founded in 1859 on the eastern slope of the Sierra Nevada near the present-day Reno following the discovery of the Comstock Lode, an extremely rich deposit of silver. The city flourished for twenty years, rivalling San Francisco with its stores, theatres, and hotels while retaining a rough frontier quality evident in its brothels, 'two-bit' saloons (25 cents per drink), dance halls, and prize fights, all memorialized in *Roughing It* (1872) by Mark Twain, who adopted that pen name while working for a Virginia City newspaper in the 1860s (see Ronald M James, *The Roar and the Silence: A History of Virginia City*, 1998). The Two Macs, mentioned also in Chapters 7 and 8, seem to be a travelling ethnic comedy team.

after scowling at Esse, turned over on her other side with a vicious dig at her pillow and an aggressive grunt. A moment later, however, the instinctive idea of duty, and work to be done, came to her, and instantly she was on her feet commencing her toilet; then Esse went out and sat by the fire, till presently her mother joined her, and later Miss Gimp, and they all fell to on the savoury breakfast which Le Maistre had ready for them.

Whilst they were eating, the Indians had struck the tent; and very shortly the little cavalcade was on its way again under the spreading aisles of the great stone-pines, and tramping with a ghostly softness on the carpet of pine needles underfoot.

The first part of the journey took them down into the valley overhung by their camping place of the night, but after crossing the stream which ran through it, they began a steady ascent which continued for hours. It was very much steeper than the ascent of the previous day, and the men all dismounted so as to relieve the ponies. Esse, too, insisted on walking, and by a sort of natural gravitation found herself at the head of the procession, walking alongside Dick, who held the rein of his pony over his arm. Hour after hour they tramped on slowly, only resting for a little while every now and again. At last, when the noon was at hand, they emerged from the forest on a bare shoulder of rock. At first the glare of the high sun dazzled Esse's eyes, focussed to the semi-gloom of the woods; but Dick and the Indians felt no such difficulty, and the former, pointing up in the direction of the Cone, said:

'Look, Little Missy. See where the tall pine rises above! There's where you're bound for, and the shaft of thet thar pine will tell you what o'clock it is.' Esse clapped her hands with delight, for the home which she had so looked forward to was in their sight. It lay on a level plateau below where the belt of verdure stopped. It was still a considerable way off, and lay some seven or eight hundred feet above them, but a fair idea could be had of its location. It was just on the northern edge of the shoulder of the great mountain,[11] and, so far as they could judge, must have a superb view. Esse was all impatience to get on, and her mother shared in her anxiety. She,

---

[11]   The lower portion of Mt Shasta does in fact extend northward to a rise called the Whaleback.

too, wanted to see in what kind of place fortune had fixed her for the months to come. From this on, the trees did not grow so densely, and here and there were patches of cleared space, where the stumps of trees, some bearing the mark of axes, and some of fire, dotted the glade. The nature of the ground did not permit of their seeing the place of destination again till, after a long spell of upward ascent, followed by a stiff bit of climbing, they emerged on the northern edge of the plateau. Then Mrs Elstree and Esse agreed that they had never seen any place so ideally beautiful.

The plateau was like an English park, ringed round with the close belt of pine forest. Great trees, singly and in clusters, rose here and there from a sward of emerald green, and through it ran a bright stream, entering from the south, and after curving by the east, fell away to the western edge of the plateau over a shelf of rock. Where the stream entered it fell from another great rock, making a waterfall sufficiently high that its spray took rainbow colours where the sunlight struck it, and fell into a great deep pool, seemingly cut by Nature's forces from the solid rock. In the centre of the plateau was a great circular hedge of prickly cactus and bear-thorn, inclosing the house in a garden of some two acres in extent. The house was small, and built solidly of logs, with a veranda all round it, and many creepers climbed over it. Right in front of its northern aspect grew a giant stone-pine, which towered up more than a hundred feet without a break, and whose wide-spreading branches threw a flickering shadow on the sward as its very height made it tremulous.

Esse was speechless, and clasped her mother's arm tightly, and then began to thump her shoulders, as had been her habit when a little child, and she had been unable in any other way to express her feelings of delight. Dick spoke:

'Well, Little Missy, ain't it a purty location; though why you should thump the old lady I don't quite see. Say, if ye want physical exercise of that kind why don't ye lam inter me! Guess I'm built more suitable fur it than that purty creetur!'

Mrs Elstree had been slightly annoyed at being spoken of as an old lady, but Dick's compliment set matters straight again, and she shook her golden head at him, and her blue eyes danced as she said:

'It's evident, Mr Grizzly, that you don't understand the feelings of a mother when her child is happy. You are not a mother!'

'Guess not!' roared Dick; 'not by a jug full!' and he slapped his thigh, and laughed with that infectious laugh of his. Esse did not altogether like to hear him laugh, especially without good cause; so to divert the subject she asked him how the tree could tell what hour it was. 'Come and see,' answered Dick, as he threw the reins of his pony to an Indian, and strode towards the house, followed eagerly by the two women, holding arms.

When they got near the hedge they turned to the right, and followed it for a little time. On the west side they found a gateway, which Dick opened. The gate seemed ridiculously massive for such a place, and was studded all over with sharp steel spikes.

'What on earth are they for?' asked Esse, pointing. The answer was as complete as it was short.

'B'ars! Things didn't uster be as they are now!' They all went inside the inclosure, and as they drew in front of the great pine Dick spread out his arms, and with a comprehensive sweep took in the whole circle of the compass. 'Look, Little Missy,' said he; tell me now what o'clock it is?' Esse looked around, and up and down, but could see no sign of any time-keeping appliance. She was disturbed by a quick little cry from her mother:

'Oh, look! Esse! look! look! the whole garden is a sun-dial!' Esse looked, and sure enough all around her, at intervals, rose groups of tall, slim pines, but at varied distances, so that there was no appearance of a ring. Some of them leaned from the perpendicular in a queer way, and yet all were so arranged that a perfect sun-dial with Roman numerals was formed, and the shadow of the great pine fell with the movement of the whirling earth, and told the tale of flying hours. There was a long pause, and Esse turned to Dick.

'Dick, did you do this?' Again the hunter slapped his thigh in mirth and his wild, resonant cachinnation seemed to sound louder than ever, as though there were some containing acoustic quality in the prickly fence. Esse got somewhat nettled, and there was a red spot on each cheek as she said:

'I don't see much to laugh at in that. I don't see why you can't answer a simple question without being rude!' Dick sobered at once, and, with a grave courtesy that seemed like a knightly act by a natural man, took off his cap and bowed his head.

'Askin' yer pardon, Little Missy. I'd no mind to be rude, nor no call to. Why, I'd not a thought of that in a thousand years. That was all done by the old doctor who found this place, and built the house, and fixed up the fence and the garden. Took a mighty deal o' pleasure in it too, seemin'ly. Every year he was here he left it less and less, till at the end he wouldn't ha' quitted, not for a farce-comedy speciality an' a comic-opera troupe rolled inter one! 'Pears to me, Little Missy, that you've come along jest in time, for there's many as would like to hev the place if onst they knowed of it.' Esse made no other reply than:

'Come along, Dick, and show me the view. I want to see the Pacific from up here.' Without a word Dick strode away to the rocky ledge over which the stream tumbled. As they got near it Miss Gimp, who had been grizzling with the indifference of all to her presence, overtook them, and said in a tone which all could hear:

'Wants to show her all the kingdoms of the earth from a high place! We know what to make of *him!*'[12] and she snorted. Esse looked at her with an amused smile, but Mrs Elstree felt annoyed, and, in order to get rid of her, asked her to go into the house and see Mrs Le Maistre, who was the housekeeper, as to the arrival. She complied with outward calmness, but was shortly afterwards seen going to the house with several Indians. One of them carried the cats, and another the dog, while a third held out at arm's length the cage of the parrot, which, from its talking, he evidently regarded with some very remarkable awe. She was letting off steam by poking the Indians in the back with the point of her umbrella. They did not resent it, but took it with that outward stoicism which marked their bearing. This aggravated her even more, and she poked the harder; but still the Indians did not resent it. She would have been not a little mortified had she known the cause of their forbearance.

Mrs Elstree and Esse stood for a long time looking at the view, and then Dick took them northward along a ledge of rock behind the belt of trees. Here there was a high, bare rock with a flat top, and on it was a natural seat of rock, resting whereon they looked round the whole horizon, except where the giant bulk of Shasta shut out the southern aspect.

Esse was in a trance of delight. Below her the mountain fell away

[12]   See the Bible, Luke 4.5-8, in which Satan tempts Jesus.

in billows of green, through which the rivers ran like threads of silver. Far away, where the whole landscape became merged in one dark, misty expanse, she could see the Pacific, a grey mass of nothingness, fringed on the near side with the jagged edge of the coast, and beyond, the arc of the horizon. Here and there in the plain hills rose and valleys dipped; but their heights and depths were lost in the distance, and had no more individual existence than the pattern of a carpet. Then she looked south, and her eye travelled up the steep side of the mountain, passing from the lessening fringe of forest to where the hardy trees stood out starkly one by one in the isolation of their strength to endure; up the rolling steep where rushes and scanty herbage grew in the shelter of the rocks; upward still, where the bare rock stood out from the grey mass of primeval rubble wherein is no vital strength, and where the snow and ice ran down in spurs into the sheltered gorges; upward still, to where the snow lay like a winding-sheet, and where the ruggedness of Nature was softened into flowing lines. And then her eye lit on the mighty curve of the mountain top, whose edges, as the high sun took them, were fringed with dazzling light. She turned to her mother, and with a sort of hysterical cry fell over against her, clasping her in her arms and hiding her tears on her bosom. 'Take me in, mother,' she said; 'I am tired, tired! and it is too sweet to see all at once!' Mrs Elstree felt her arms relax, and bent down anxiously; Esse had fainted. The mother knew of her long illness, and was not altogether surprised, but Dick was overcome with anxiety, as strong natural men are where womankind and her weakness are concerned, and he said, in an awe-struck whisper:

'The poor, purty little thing! Let me carry her for ye, marm. I'll bear her very gently!' Mrs Elstree nodded, and he took her up in his powerful arms as though she was a baby, and together they went softly to the house.

At the door they were met by the entire household with Mrs Le Maistre at the head; Miss Gimp rushed out on seeing the body of Esse carried limply, and began to scream and call out:

'Is she dead? Is it an accident? Oh, my child, my child!' and she beat her hands wildly together. Miss Gimp was a good creature in spite of her eccentricity, and Grizzly Dick summed her up fairly when he said: 'The old girl is a crank from Crankville; but her heart is in the right lo-cation all the same.' Mrs Elstree tried to soothe her, and raised her hand as she said:

'Hush, hush! she has only fainted. The journey and the hot sun have been too much for her. She will be all right presently!' Then Mrs Le Maistre, who had been her nurse, took her in her strong arms, and carried her in, not without protest from Dick.

'Let me carry her, marm. Purty Little Missy, I'll be as gentle as her mother!' As they entered the doorway Esse opened her eyes, and, after looking at them all for a few seconds, in a dazed sort of way, said suddenly, whilst a bright blush took the place of her pallor:

'Oh, let me down, I'm all right now! Don't let Dick see me like this; he'll think me a baby!' Miss Gimp sniffed as she looked over at Dick, but said nothing, for it was borne in upon her, swiftly but conclusively, that he was a mighty fine figure of a man.

Towards evening, when, after a lie down and a cup of tea, Esse was feeling quite restored, she asked her mother if she might go out and see the sunset. Without a word, Mrs Elstree tied a scarf over her head, for the evening was growing chilly at this altitude, and taking her daughter's arm they strolled out towards the entrance gate and across the plateau. Once more they sat upon the rocky seat and looked out westward. Once again they saw the sun sink, a red globe, into the western sea, and the dark shadow of night climb up the hill-side, and the summit of Shasta gleam ghostly white.

And then they went in.

THREE

FOR several weeks the life on the Shasta was ideal, and Mrs Elstree's heart rejoiced to see the changes it was working in Esse. Her languidness seemed to have disappeared, and she was now bright, brisk, and alert, for ever devising new ways of passing the time, and helping with invention and design to improve the place. Le Maistre, who had a pretty mechanical aptitude of his own, had designed a new water supply for the house, and was already carrying it into execution. From the rocky basin which stood up the mountain nearly three hundred feet above the house, he was to lay a series of logs, pierced with great augers, now being brought up from San Francisco on purpose. These were to be joined together, and would convey so easily applicable as well as so abundant a supply that Esse had designed several fountains for round the house, each of which would throw up a fair sheet of water to a considerable height. Thus from whatever way the wind blew, something of the cooling spray could be borne to the house. In this work Dick was of great use, not only by his lending a hand himself, but by being able to induce the Indians to help. A few nondescript settlers of lower down the mountain were glad to earn a little money, and altogether muscular power was not wanting. Dick was only present now and again, for his hunting pursuits took him away sometimes for a few days at a time. But his time was not wasted in so far as the household was concerned, for it was he who kept the larder supplied with fresh meat. There was always abundance of all sorts of game, and a very liberal supply of necessaries had been laid in; the garden afforded a good supply of fruit and vegetables, and altogether no need for comfort was lacking.

Esse's great amusement was with the Indians. She very soon learned that their village was in a deep cleft which lay between the house and the western side of the mountain.[1] As a little rocky peak

---

[1]   Historically the Indians living in the area surrounding Mt Shasta were Shastas to the

lay between them, it was not possible to see even the smoke of their fires. On the near side to them, but on the far side of the rock, Dick's cabin stood on a rocky shelf beside a spring. From it he could see the whole western slope of the mountain, and by it he could on his many journeys make for the most direct way home. His proximity kept the Indians in order; for with the dominance of a Caucasian he made himself to some degree regulator of his neighbour's affairs. Indeed, he stood with regard to the Indians somewhat in the relation of a British justice of the peace to the village community.[2] This dominance was a great comfort to Mrs Elstree, who had at the first some doubts as to the physical security of her party, removed so far as they were from any means of help. An incident which occurred shortly after her arrival had not tended to allay her fears.

She had been taking a siesta in a hammock slung between two of the sun-dial trees, and was in the semi-lethargic condition of one who is sleeping for mere luxury, not need – such a sweetly overpowering condition as is only to be felt in the open air – when she noticed one of the Indians approach stealthily. He was one of the most brainless looking of the tribe, and in general a sort of butt of the rest. His face was in fact only removed a degree above idiocy, and this by the cunning twinkle of his eyes. His character, as it often happens amongst Indians, was shown in his name, Hi'-oh', which means Heap (or always) Hungry in the Shoshonie dialect.[3]

---

north, west, and south; Achomawis to the southeast; and Modocs to the northeast. The Indians of the American West were overwhelmed during the nineteenth century, especially after the Gold Rush of 1849, by the huge influx of farmers, prospectors, miners, and hunters from the eastern United States. Indian resistance broke out particularly in the 1850s through the 1870s but was in general eliminated by treaties and armed force which resulted in the removal of most surviving Indians to reservations. The Indians of the Mt Shasta area were in the main transferred to reservations in the 1850s and 1860s, and in 1872-73 a Modoc rebellion was defeated and its leader, 'Captain Jack,' was executed. Although most northern California Indians were in reservations by the 1890s, some, according to Howard Lamar's *New Encyclopedia of the American West* (1998), 'fled to the interior, maintaining primitive, backland enclaves against the Anglos.'

[2]   The British justice of the peace preserved the peace in a county, town, or other district by deciding and punishing in minor cases of lawbreaking and by presenting serious cases for trial by a judge and jury.

[3]   'Shoshonie' is usually spelled 'Shoshone.' Historically the Indians of the Mt Shasta area were not Shoshones and did not speak their language, Uto-Aztecan. The Modocs spoke Penutian; the Shastas and Achomawis spoke Hokan. The Shoshones lived in

Half amused, and half in that adventurous state of mind when fear
becomes a sort of intellectual tickling – a sort of continuation of her
dreams – Mrs Elstree lay still, pretending slumber. He approached
with increasing stealthiness, keeping always behind some tree
trunk, till he had reached the head of the hammock. Now, when he
was out of her sight, Mrs Elstree became seriously alarmed, but by a
great effort she lay still, though her heart beat like a trip-hammer.
The seconds seemed to be years, and in the agonizing suspense she
could hear – or thought she could – the blood running through the
veins of her neck. Then slowly and cautiously a pair of copper-
coloured hands stole gently down the netting of the hammock, and
with deft movement the fingers began inserting themselves under
her head. With a tremendous effort she lay quite still, for she felt
that it was too late now to do anything if harm to her were
intended. Her only grain of consolation – and it necessitated a new
effort to suppress the smile which it caused – was that her scalp
would be different from the general run of such curios. She had
once seen, in a chest full of scalps, in the collection of a friend who
was an amateur of Indian trophies, a scalp of a woman's golden
hair, and she herself, in common with all who had seen it, felt more
pity for the late owner of those yellow tresses, than for all the
original proprietors of the dark ones put together. She could in her
mind's eye see her own tresses hanging up in a wigwam, or helping
to trim a buck's festal costume, and already she had begun to hope
that his earth-colours would match her hair. Here her thoughts
were cut short by a strange sensation. The hands were lifting her
head and holding it balanced; then it was laid down again softly,
and the hands were withdrawn. Once more she conquered a strong
impulse to start up, for she thought it better not to appear to have
noticed. So she lay still awhile, breathing softly. Then she yawned,

central Wyoming and in the area between the Rockies and the Sierra Nevada. By the late
nineteenth century, most had been concentrated in reservations in Wyoming and Idaho,
while some remained in scattered locations in Nevada and southern California's Death
Valley area according to D H Thomas and others in 'Western Shoshones' in *Handbook
of North American Indians* (*HNAI*), vol 11 (1996). The novel's purported Shoshone
words here and later on do not correspond with relevant terms in Shoshone vocabularies
published by Wick R Miller in the *HNAI*, vol 17 (1996), George W Hill (1877), and Jon
P Dayley (1989).

raised her arms, turned over, and as if waking, assumed a sitting
posture. She looked around keenly; but there was no sign of an
Indian about the place.

At first she was a little startled, and then a queer kind of doubt
came upon her as to whether she had not been asleep and dreamed
the whole thing. As there was no trace of an Indian, she remained
in doubt, not liking to tell any one, lest it might cause ill feeling.
Dick was away; but the day after he returned, and she took the
opportunity of being alone with him to ask his opinion of the
transaction. To her surprise, but also to her relief, Dick burst into
his characteristic roar of laughter.

'Wall, durn my skin!' said he, 'but that is the all-firedest funniest
rascal I ever kem across. I guess now what was in Heap Hungry's
thick head when he made a proposition to me that we should work
a gold mine together: "Hi'-oh' knows," sez he, "of a gold mine,
much gold on top. If much gold on top, mucher gold under that,
waugh!" He is a cunnin' beggar, too; wouldn't take any chances
over his gold mine, but wanted to make cert if it was gold.'

'But I don't understand!' said Mrs Elstree. Dick slapped his
thigh again in his emphatic way, and roared with laughter:

'Why, marm, don't ye see. You was the gold mine! With the
golden hair atop, he thought as how yer skull would be gold, an' he
wanted to make sure before ringin' me in, so's we'd kill you
together and wash up fair!' Mrs Elstree shuddered, but she laughed
nevertheless; she felt when Dick took so grim a thing jocularly it
would not do for her to make new troubles.

But she was seriously disturbed in her mind all the same. She
was not accustomed to Indians, and their ways and their proximity,
combined with the possibilities of such ideas as had been brought to
her notice, made her anxious. It might be all very well to have a
terrible penalty afterwards exacted by one's friends; but scalping
was not a pleasant matter to contemplate, and the battle between
the edge of a tomahawk and the human skull was not altogether a
fair one.

Esse got on very well with the Indians. They had the idea that
she was somehow or other under the special protection of Dick,
and she was herself so kind to them, that to show her their
eagerness to serve came easy. At first they amused her, and then,

when she knew them a little better, they disgusted her. In fact, she went with them through somewhat of those phases with which one comes to regard a monkey before its place in the scale of creation is put in true perspective. Now and again she grew furiously indignant when there came under her notice some instance of their habitual and brutal cruelty to their squaws and children, their dogs and their horses. At first she used to speak to Dick, and to please her he would rate and threaten them; but she soon began to see that this was not quite fair to the hunter, as it created a certain sullenness towards him, which augured badly for future peace. So she gradually began to realize that, in spite of their ragged relics of a higher civilization, they were but little better than savages, and with the savage instincts which could not be altered all at once.[4] Dick, who was, like all hunters, a close observer of little things, noticed the change in her bearing, and spoke of it in his own frank way:

'Guess, Little Missy, you're gettin' the hang of the Indian. He ain't of much account nohow, and ye can't bet money on him more'n on a yaller dog. Though he ain't so bad as those think that don't know him. There's times when the cruelty of that lot of ours makes me so mad, I want to wipe them all out; but I know all the same that there isn't one of them, man, woman, or child, that wouldn't stand between me and death. Ay, or between any of you and death either. Guess, you're about beginnin' to size up the noble red man without his frills!'

The member of the party who got on best with the Indians was Miss Gimp. Le Maistre they respected and looked up to on account of his big beard; and for Mrs Le Maistre they had the respect and affection which goes with the enjoyment of toothsome delicacies. But Miss Gimp ruled amongst them like a princess. No matter how she rated them for their imperfect costume, or their dirty ways, or their cruelty, they never made reply except their grave obeisance; and the point of her umbrella made, without evoking remonstrance, indentations in their bodies. Whenever they saw her stiff

---

[4]   Sources such as the *Dictionary of Indian Tribes of the Americas* (1980) provide little historical corroboration for Esse's characterization of the Shasta-area Indians. Whereas the novel usually presents seemingly unchangeable anthropological characterizations, Esse allows for gradual improvement of the Indians from 'savage instincts' to 'higher civilization.'

skirts moving along the sward – for Miss Gimp adhered loyally to the traditions of her youth and wore hoops – albeit of an undefined pattern – they would glide up as near as they could, keeping furtively in the shelter of the trees. So long as they were allowed, they would hang around her, looking like a lot of spectres who had seen better days. At first this used to annoy her, but it very soon became a source of pride, for human nature very soon becomes accustomed to the deference of inferiors. Miss Gimp, in her mind, regarded them as in some sort a kind of royal cohort, and began to treat them with added disdain, such as is supposed to be the attribute of royalty. They were perpetually sneaking round the house, and if they saw her at a window would wait patiently for hours in the hope of her coming out. Both Mrs Elstree and Esse saw with amusement this perpetual attention on their part, but never said anything to her about it. Esse noticed that it used to give the most intense amusement to Dick whenever he chanced to see it, and that he often hurried away with a purple face; and she, listening, would hear the forest echoing to his explosive laughter. One day she followed him and came upon him sitting upon the trunk of a fallen tree, slapping his thighs, and with his long hair tossing about as he shook his head in a paroxysm of laughter. He did not hear her approach, and for a few moments she stood looking at him, at first a little indignant that he should be making such a fool of himself; but then the contagion of his laughter took her, and she too burst out in a wild peal. He instantly started to his feet, all his instincts of protection and aggression awake, and for the moment sobered into a grim seriousness. When, however, he saw who it was, the lines of his face relaxed, and he said:

'Wall, an' it's you, Little Missy. Durn! if I hadn't kem away by myself I'd have busted – jest busted with laughter. The old lady takes the Indians like she was a queen, an' all the while it ain't her they're after at all. There ain't one of them that wouldn't take and put a tomahawk through her skull or skelp her so far as the queenin' racket is concerned.'

'Then what is it they are after, Dick?'

'It's the parrot! Nothin' else than that durned parrot!' and again Dick went off into fits of laughter. When he recovered his breath, he went on:

'Did ye notice him lately – the parrot, I mean – they've all been tryin' to get near him, and jest now one of them went up nigh him, an' as soon as he got near up, the durned bird says "How!" jest as well as if he was a Christian or an Indian. The man was so took back that he was like to drop. They all thought he was a god before, but nothin' in this world would make them disbelieve it now!'

'But how does this affect Miss Gimp?'

'Why, don't ye see, Little Missy, that she has the charge of him; she's the sachem,[5] the medicine-man, the witch, and they want to make themselves solid with her because they think she can square him. There isn't one of them that likes her; but, all the same, they'd go a good length to please old Yam-pi, as they call her.'

'What is Yam-pi? What does it mean?' said Esse, inquisitively.

'It means, in Shoshonie, "Leather Legs," or "the old woman with boots,"'[6] said Dick, and he laughed again.

Esse came away from the wood not altogether pleased with Dick. There seemed to be an overpowering levity in his character which did not altogether suit her idea of him, based originally on his fine physique. A woman who likes a man wants to respect him, and as Dick was the only male in the place, for of course Indians and servants did not count, she felt that she had to think of him now and then.

One morning Miss Gimp was in a state of suppressed excitement which at once arrested Esse's attention. At breakfast she could not remain still, but buzzed and fluttered about everyone and everything in an unusual way. Mrs Elstree with her usual placidity did not notice anything out of the common, or, if she did, kept it to herself. Esse had therefore the sweet interest of a secret, and she carefully noticed every detail of the companion, and very shortly came to the conclusion that she had a secret which she was simply bursting to tell someone – anyone. With true feminine perversity she therefore, at once and sternly, made up her mind that she would not assist in the unfolding at all. If Gimp wanted to tell

---

[5]   A sachem, strictly defined, is a 'band' leader or tribal chief among the Algonquin-speaking Indians of southern New England.

[6]   'Yam-pi' is intriguingly close to the Shoshone *nampih* ('shoe'), but, for example, in Shoshone vocabularies (see note 3) 'boot' is *to-ho-namp* and *poqtssi*; 'old woman' is *hippico* and *hipittsi*; and 'leg' is *mah-omb* and *nung-kwappuh*.

anything she would have to do so altogether on her own initiative. It would of course have been quite a different thing if Gimp had a secret which she didn't want to tell; in such case Esse would have had to make the overtures and do the entire corkscrew business herself. Therefore it was that the games of hide-and-seek, run-away-and-follow, were so prolonged that morning until they would have afforded the most exquisite enjoyment to any third party who had been in the secret. Esse stayed all the early forepart of the morning with her mother, nothing could take her away, lured Miss Gimp never so wisely; and when she did go out it was at a time when Miss Gimp was absorbed in some household duty and could not follow her. She went into the wood, and when Miss Gimp followed and called after her softly, she did not answer; so hour after hour Miss Gimp had to bear in her breast the burden of her untold secret. After lunch Esse's heart relented, and she strolled out to the seat on the rocks so that Miss Gimp could follow her. She sat down, and within a few minutes the amanuensis sat alongside her and had entered on her theme. Esse noticed that she had put on a veil, an adornment – or concealment – so rare with her that it became at once noticeable. Esse sat down and waited. She had allowed the first step to be taken and had to be wooed into accepting the next. Miss Gimp looked up at her under her eyelids with a very tolerable imitation of bashfulness, simpered, sighed, looked up and down several times, turned warily round to see that there was no one else within earshot, gave a premonitory cough, and opened proceedings:

'It is a very strange thing!' said she.

'Indeed?'

'Yes, my dear; and the worst of it is that it is so embarrassing. One doesn't wish to make anyone unhappy, much less to ruin their lives!' After a pause, which Esse filled up with another 'Indeed,' Miss Gimp went on:

'I have been told that young men take such matters so to heart that they grow wild, and go out and drink, and do all manner of dreadful things!' Esse's curiosity was now becoming interested; she had a vague idea that Miss Gimp had some kind of hallucination as to a love affair, but she could not quite make out yet what was its special direction. She felt herself thinking a phrase which she had several times heard Dick use, 'How many kinds of a durn'd fool was it that she was makin' of herself?' Her monotonous 'Indeed' was hardly adequate to the situation, so she added with as little tendency towards laughter as she could manage.

'Poor young man! You must not let him suffer too much!' Miss Gimp sighed and wiped a phantom tear from her cheek as she said in a far-away manner.

'Oh, poor Dick! Poor dear Dick! I fear he has much suffering before him! – Did you speak?' she added in a different tone, for Esse had on the instant been taken with a sudden and very violent cough which made her in a short space of time grow almost purple in the face. The shock was too much when Miss Gimp apostrophized the man who was the victim of unhappy attachment, and in her mind's eye rose the burly figure of Grizzly Dick, driven crazed for love, painting red spots all over the town of Sacramento. The figure changed instantly to the same man sitting amongst the forest trees, slapping his thighs and roaring with laughter as he thought of Miss Gimp and the parrot, and the relative places which they held in Indian esteem. Miss Gimp bridled somewhat, and seemed more than ever to justify her Indian name; but Esse, who really liked her, found her risibility checked by her genuine concern for her, apologized for the interruption, and asked her to go on. So, with as many 'flirts and flutters' as Poe's famous bird of ill omen,[7] Miss Gimp began her story.

'It has surprised – surprised me very much, to find little offerings placed outside my window. Most odd things, my dear – wild turkeys and young fawns, hare, bear-meat, and sometimes fruit of an edible kind, potatoes, honey, and such like. I wondered who could have put them there!' Here she simpered in a way that would have looked artificial in a girls' school on the day when male relatives are received. Then she went on with marked inconsequentiality:

'It would be a sin – a perfect sin to drive to desperation such a fine figure of a man!' Esse had expected to find her laughter uncontrollable as the story went on, but instead she felt something beginning to overpower her which was much nigher akin to tears. How

---

[7]   In lines 37-38 of 'The Raven' by Edgar Allan Poe (1809-1849) a student has heard a tapping at his window and opened it, and, 'with many a flirt and flutter, / In there stepped a stately Raven.'

could she but feel sorrow for the poor, dear old thing who with all her oddities was as loyal and as true as the sunlight. She knew that whatever was the cause of her error, there was no possibility of her manifest wishes being carried out. Then came a doubt. 'How did she herself know this?' with the consequent answer, 'Because Dick was already' – the thought was completed in her mind with an overpowering rush of blood to her face, which Miss Gimp must have noticed only that she was coyly turning away and simpering all to herself.

It is commonly thought that men and women become transformed and glorified in and by great moments. This may be so, but the common idea of great moments is not so true to Nature. There are great moments for all the Children of Adam; but they are not always great through the force of external facts. The dramatic moment in real life does not always come amongst picturesque and suitable surroundings. It is the conjuncture of spiritual and mundane suitabilities which makes the opportunity of the dramatist; but to others, who are the puppets of the great dramatic poet Nature, the moments of transfiguration come as they came to St Paul.[8] The Great Light which turns the thoughts of men inwards, and reveals to themselves the secret springs of their own actions, has many moral and psychical and intellectual manifestations. The pagans whose imagination wrought into existence the whole theology of Olympus, had a subtle insight into the human heart when they showed the familiar figure of Cupid shooting his sweetly poisoned arrows at them that slept.

Such a crucial moment was now for Esse. She had come to that great temple of the hillside to laugh – to laugh at the brain-sick, love-sick fancies of an old woman whose whole being seemed a mockery of the possibilities of love; and she had remained to pray, with a bitter pang of hope and fear. In the whirling of her thought she got glimpses into her own soul which made her cheeks burn, even while half in a fainting mood she felt the solid earth slipping beneath her feet. Her mind must have been earnestly occupied, for

8   See the Bible, Acts 22.1-11, which relates Paul's totally unexpected conversion from Judaism to Christianity by a sudden manifestation of light and the voice of Jesus while Paul was going to Damascus to take charge of some Christian prisoners and deliver them to Jerusalem for punishment.

she did not hear Miss Gimp go on with her story. It was strange to her that after a pause of mental blankness, during which she sat still, she felt the roaring in her ears pass away and realized that Miss Gimp was speaking – speaking with the volubility of one who has entered on a congenial theme and is under its sway:

'Of course, my dear, Dick being a hunter thinks that he should make his – he! he! – offerings of a suitable kind. It is most embarrassing, for a girl can't put a leg of a deer, or a bear ham, or a wild turkey, into a jewel case, or lock it up in a drawer, so that she can take it out when no one is looking and kiss it. In fact there is no sense in kissing a ham or a leg of raw meat at all, and if you lock it up in a drawer it doesn't smell very nice, even if it does not go bad altogether. The matter is now getting serious. I assure you, my dear, that my room is beginning to get into a shocking state. I am positively afraid to open the lower section of my chest of drawers, for I put the first of the – the offerings in there; and there's a very suspicious odour from it already. I wish you'd advise me, my dear, what I ought to do!' There was such a delightful air of seriousness about Miss Gimp as she made her strange disclosure, and it seemed so absolutely out of harmony with the ridiculous matter, that Esse felt once more an almost overpowering desire to laugh. She felt that she could not overcome it if she remained where she was, so she started up briskly, and, taking Miss Gimp by the arm, called out:

'Come along quick! – We must look over the jewel casket, and see what can be done.' Miss Gimp would rather have sat still and nursed her sentiment, but she was overborne by Esse's spirits and energy; and so hand in hand, like a pair of children, they raced to the house.

When they went into Miss Gimp's room there was no possibility of mistaking the odour. Even a properly arranged larder is not always the most pleasant of places, but a lady's bedroom is in no way adapted for the storage of dead flesh. Esse for a moment felt qualmish, and would have decamped at once only that Miss Gimp had silently and mysteriously locked the door, and so she remained, supported solely by the humour of the situation. Miss Gimp walked on tip-toe over to the chest of drawers and opened the top drawer. 'Here is the last,' she said as she lovingly surveyed a fine wild turkey which was huddled into the drawer, wings and neck and tail twisted about ruthlessly. She put in her hand and began to stroke its feathers, whilst she sighed pensively. The idea of a hunter's bride was strongly fixed in her mind, and with it a tenderness towards all belonging to his craft. Esse now wanted to see the job over so she asked:

'And where is the first?' Miss Gimp pulled out the lowest drawer of all and disclosed to Esse's gaze a horrible looking leg of deer meat all blue, damp and sodden; and which had been rudely hacked from the carcase. The look and the smell almost turned Esse faint, and with a sudden jerk she shut up the drawer. 'What an awful thing to send you!' was all she could say. Miss Gimp was pathetically apologetic in her manner as she said:

'Well, it is an odd way of showing affection. If it had been a nice gold specimen now, or one of those opals in the matrix, like the one that was presented to your mother in Mexico, or a slab of onyx, one would understand it better. But the dear man has his own ways I suppose! He is a fine figure of a man, isn't he?' This she said in a burst of something like rapture. Esse tried to cut this short – the new light still shone round her enough to make it seem unfair to let the other woman show her heart, more especially when her hopes were so baseless; so she turned the conversation to what was to be done with the offerings. Miss Gimp was beginning to be seriously alarmed about being found out, on one side as hoarding the provisions in such a ridiculous way, and on the other of being laughed at if she broached the subject at all; so she was glad to embrace Esse's suggestion that they should during the darkness of the evening take out the gifts and bury them.

This fell deed was achieved before they went to bed that night, and Miss Gimp slept peacefully, with the consciousness of a weight taken off her mind.

The next morning Esse came across Dick, who was for once in a way in a tearing rage. She asked him the cause, and he told her:

'It's that durned crowd – dirty, thievin' scoundrels; an' I believe that Heap Hungry is at the bottom of it. I'd make some of them own up, but that it don't suit me to quarrel with them just now. I'll lay for them some night an' I'll put a hole through some of them.'

'What have they been stealing?'

'Not much – nothin' of any value, but it's the beginnin', and I mean to stop it right here. An Indian is real pizon when he gets off the square, and this may be only one in the lot; but it's a beginnin', and I won't stand it!' Esse began to have an understanding, so she asked again:

'What did they steal, Dick?'

'Oh, only some meat and such like. A week ago I had a buck hangin' up, an' in the night the durned thieves came and hacked a leg off it; last night it was a turkey. By gum, Little Missy, what air you laughin' at now?' for Esse had gone off in peals of laughter after his own manner. At first he was annoyed, but in a few seconds the anger of his face disappeared; then his features relaxed into a grin and the pent up whirlwind burst, and Esse's laughter was drowned in the volume of his stentorian tones. When Esse recovered her breath she told him what she had found out, and as Dick's laughter broke out afresh at every step of the doing, of Heap Hungry's stealing the meat and placing it in Miss Gimp's window as an offering to the parrot, of her taking it to herself and as a love gift from Dick, and of the mysterious burying. Then she suggested that to complete the circle Dick should come each night and dig up the offering and use it either for himself or for Mrs Elstree's household. The humour of the idea took hold of Dick, and his imagination was so manifestly touched that Esse got a little frightened lest he should in some way betray the secret. She was only made easy when he solemnly swore not to betray the secret in any way.

And so this night Dick went to his cabin shaking with laughter; and Esse put her head on her pillow filled with a secret but fearful exultation that Dick and she shared a secret between them.

FOUR

ESSE'S first quarrel with Dick arose from wounded vanity.
Remotely the feeling may have been on his side, but the
immediate cause was on her own part. When the secret had
been shared for some time, she began to take Dick to task in a
purely feminine way. She wanted his hands to be always clean, and
his nails to be properly regulated. Dick was something of a dandy in
his way, but in the mountains vanity prefers more picturesque
forms than the manifestations of soap and water. He was not by any
means a dirty man; but more than the mere absence of dirt is
demanded by the exigence of feminine propinquity, and Esse,
greatly daring, took him to task. He received her monitions well
enough at the time, but later on developed a certain huffiness
which told her that his self-love had been wounded. Anxious to set
matters right, she took an early opportunity of saying to him:

'Dick, you know you and I should help one another. You are big
and strong, and mother says that the care you have taken of me,
and the sense of security which your presence gives has made a new
girl of me. I want to see you like other men – no, no! I don't mean
like them, with all their meanness and selfishness, but in not being
ridiculous or not seeming at your best. Down in the cities men have
rules among themselves as to how they should dress and what they
should do; and I wouldn't like any of them to misjudge you, if you
should be there, or they here. You're not offended with me, are
you, Dick?' He had been sitting with his knees apart and his face
downcast, but there was something in her voice which made him
look up. His great blue eyes looked into her great brown ones, and
the whole quarrel was made up in one word as he held out his great
brown hand and said:

'Shake!' Esse took the pleasant punishment of his pump-handle
shake without a wince, and when Dick had dropped her hand as
suddenly as he had grasped it she felt in a less dictatorial mood
towards him than she had ever experienced. With a certain new

shyness she said:

'And I want you, Dick, to tell me of anything you notice that isn't quite right in me – not quite as you'd have it in a girl that you respected. You know, Dick, we all want help to do the best that we are capable of!' she went on in a voice that somehow seemed to herself not to ring true, though Dick did not seem to notice it. He fidgetted his hands about awkwardly and blushed, actually blushed like a school-girl – that is, as a school-girl is supposed to blush according to the books. Then he coughed prefatorily: this sent a pang through Esse's heart, or whatever portion of her anatomy vanity resides in. Did a woman ever yet not feel a pang when a man whom she liked discovered the smallest fault? She could have beaten herself for the falsity of her tone as she said, with seeming impulsiveness:

'Go on, Dick! Don't be afraid! I'll tell you if you're right.' So Dick began:

'Wall, Little Missy, as you wish me to tell you, there is a matter – I don't know as how I oughter mention it; or I don't quite know how to say it right. But it hasn't been my own noticin' entirely. Them Shoshonies are mighty cute[1] in noticin', an' they have a name for you which tells it; or rather they had, till I promised to knock the stuffin' out of any of them that would use it again.'

'What was it?' asked Esse in curiosity, though her face was suffused with an indignant blush. But Dick kept an artful silence on the point.

'Well, Little Missy, I think I'd better explain to you first. Why do you keep that nose-rag of yours always over your face the way you do? Guess, it looks mighty odd to folks!' Esse's blush turned a bright scarlet; she had a habit which had adhered to her from childhood up, just as some children maintain the habit of sucking the thumb, and concerning which she had often been spoken to and remonstrated with. She would twirl her handkerchief round her forefinger and thumb, and then place these fingers, parted widely, across her nose and mouth and sit reading hour after hour in this attitude. Even when she was not reading she would unconsciously assume the same position. She could not but be

---

[1]   Acute.

conscious that the habit was an odd one even if her mother and Miss Gimp had not kept her eternally informed of it, and it was simply gall and wormwood to her to have Dick notice the matter and join in the ranks of her tormentors. For a few moments she remained silent in sheer bewilderment as to what she should say, and then the only thing that was possible under the circumstances was spoken:

'Thank you! Dick, it is a bad habit I know, and mother and Gimp are always hammering me about it. I suppose I got into a habit as a child, and it has stuck to me. But I'll try and get rid of it! indeed I will.' There were tears of mortified vanity in her eyes, which recognizing, Dick held out a red hand and gave his comfort in a homeopathic[2] dose:

'Shake!' Then Esse grew coy and said:

'Not till you tell me what the Indians call me.' Dick looked for a moment embarrassed, and then his laugh rang out.

'Ha! ha! ha! Well, Little Missy, I'll tell you – they call you Pahoo-mounon-he-ka.'

'And what does that mean?' As she spoke Esse tried to keep down her flaming indignation. The very fact of her not knowing what the word or phrase meant intensified her feeling. *Omne ignotum pro magnifico.*[3] Dick answered:

'It means, "Nose-ghost";[4] so you see that even the Shoshonies, that haven't had a nose-rag among them since Adam, noticed that you don't use yours correctly.'

'I presume that you mean a pocket-handkerchief by – by that – that vulgar phrase,' said Esse tartly.

---

[2]   Homeopathic medicine treats its patient for the symptom of a disease by administering a minute dose of a substance that would produce a similar symptom in a healthy person. Dick remedies Esse's tears with a handshake that six paragraphs earlier has made her 'wince.'

[3]   Latin for 'everything unknown is considered marvelous,' from Tacitus, *Agricola* 30, in which a northern Scots chieftain in 83 AD states the quoted maxim and tells his forces that hitherto their remoteness from Roman Britain and their 'obscure renown' have protected them from invasion, but now they must prepare for it because the Romans, led by Agricola, have marched northward past the farthest boundary of Britain.

[4]   The Shoshone vocabularies cited in note 3, Chapter 3, list provocative but by no means exact matches for elements of 'Pahoo-mounon-he-ka': for 'ghost,' *poha*; and for 'nose,' *mupin.*

'That's so. But look here, Little Missy, since we're on the trail, and we mean to run down the game this time – and since you kick – oh, yes, you do! Don't I see it in every corner of your face! A man don't learn woodcraft without gettin' to notice little things like that! Let us wash up clean right here. Why do you always carry the nose-rag – excuse me little Missy, the pocket-handkerchief – rolled up in a ball when you're not making a tent of it over your nose?'

'I don't do anything of the kind!' said Esse indignantly, and again the tears of mortified vanity rose in her eyes. Dick laughed in a way that seemed more insulting and aggressive than ever as he slapped his thigh in the way that aggravated Esse more than anything else.

'Wall, bust me if that doesn't take the cake! Here is you denyin' that; an' all the time you're a-holdin' your nose-rag screwed up just the same as ever!' Esse looked at her hand, and, seeing the handkerchief just as he had said, flung it on the ground as though it had been something noxious. Then, turning her back, she ran out of the glade, and went home.

An hour later she went back to the glade to get the handkerchief, but she could not find it; it had gone. From this little fact she felt that Miss Gimp could have woven a romance; and somehow it did not seem to her that it would have been quite ridiculous on the part of Miss Gimp.

Two days afterwards, Dick, in the midst of a conversation, suddenly stopped and handed her the handkerchief, neatly washed out and folded:

'This belongs to you, Little Missy. You dropped it in the wood the other night when you ran away.' Esse took it with a simple 'thank you,' but when she got home, she put it in the locked drawer where she kept her valuables of all sorts.

The constant habit of trying to conquer her old trick when Dick was present seemed in some way to make a subtle kind of barrier between them. But it was in truth only a subtle barrier, and one that thought could overleap at will. The very existence of such a restraint raised the rough man in the girl's eyes to a more important position, and blinded her to a thousand little roughnesses and coarsenesses which would have hourly offended her more cultured susceptibilities. This very lack of refinement on Dick's part caused

Esse many unhappy moments, for he seemed to fail to see that she was trying her best to rid herself of the ridiculous habit, and would often notice failures to which a more delicately minded person would have been wilfully blind. Thus, Esse soon grew to abandon the habit of covering her mouth and nose, but she still instinctively and unconsciously clung to the habit of rolling her handkerchief, and keeping it hidden in the hollow of her hand. But habits, be they never so trivial or ridiculous, have a hideous vitality of their own, and Esse soon found to her cost, that this unutterably trivial habit, which both the Indians and the trapper had noticed, had a tenacity denied to worthier things. She was often wounded to the quick when Dick, in his boisterous way would notice her resumption of her failing; but all the time this little trial was forming her character and developing that consciousness of effort which marks the border line between girl and woman. Once she was goaded into a retort – but such a retort as she had never dreamed of – when Dick had slapped his thigh, and with a Titanic peal of laughter remarked:

'Wall, Little Missy, the Ghost is kep' to home in the shanty to-day, but she's sent the wean[5] on the trail!' She answered, with a certain soft appealing in her voice:

'You needn't be too hard on me, Dick. I am doing my best; but I can't be quite perfect all at once.' She had never in all her life been so sweetly womanly as at the moment, and even whilst she spoke she could not but feel that some change had taken place in her own nature. Dick seemed to realize this too, for off came his cap in a moment in apology, and he said with, for him, gravity:

'Your pardon, Little Missy. Why, I wouldn't pain you for all the world!' Esse smiled, and held out her hand, which was by this time nearly as brown as his own, and said, in exact imitation of his style, 'Shake!' And so that breeze passed on its way and left the air clearer behind it.

In these days Miss Gimp was nursing a gentle melancholy, which was daily fostered on game, honey, and raw meat, which took their usual course on their allotted circle from Dick's larder to Miss Gimp's window-sill, thence, *via* her wardrobe, to the place of burial,

---

[5]   Apparently this is the Scots 'wean,' meaning 'wee one, child.'

and so back to the larder again. Heap Hungry was more than ever assiduous in his attentions to the parrot, and was maturing schemes of his own. Esse had now taken up her sketching, and having exhausted all the picturesque possibilities of the plateau, had begun to go further afoot in search of material to suit her fancy. Tired of the endless expanse, she now sought inclosed dells amidst the woods. She used to go about alone now, for her health had been completely restored by the bracing air, and the chemical qualities of the water, as the doctors had foretold. She sometimes took the dog with her, but not always; for the freedom of the mountain had somewhat demoralized it, and it took to hunting in miniature on its own account, instead of devoting itself solely to the wishes of its mistress. At first Miss Gimp used to accompany her, but Esse got so unutterably tired of her perpetual chattering, that by-and-by she began to make excuses to leave her at home. When she found that these, being naturally limited, began to be exhausted, she kept her away by making her own sketching tours to distant places. Miss Gimp knew when she was beaten in this respect, and after a time made no effort to accompany her. Esse had by this time, under Dick's guidance, learned to shoot with a heavy revolver, which he insisted that she should always carry with her when out of sight of the house.

"Tain't, Little Missy, that I'm afeard of any special harm; because if I'm put to it I can't point out any as is likely to come. But in the forest everythin' or anythin' may be harmful, and you can't be wrong anyhow in bein' heeled[6] proper! Some day or other you'll find that very derringer[7] of yourn the best friend you ever set eyes on. But even if ye don't, wall! then the exercise of carryin' it won't do your muscles no harm!' Mrs Elstree did not at first like the idea of Esse carrying firearms, but when she saw that she soon acquired a certain dexterity in their use she solaced herself with the thought that at any rate they meant protection.

One day Esse, straying further than usual down the steep side of the mountain, came to a spot which excited all her artistic

---

[6]   Armed.
[7]   Strictly and literally, 'derringer' designates a small, short-barreled pistol with a large bore, effective at short range, taking its name from its inventor, the Philadelphia gunsmith Henry Deringer (1786-1868), with the addition of the second r by a journalist.

admiration. The hot sun beat into a dell so well watered that even in the great heat the grass was as green as emerald, and there was about everything a semi-tropical luxuriance. There was a fallen tree, which served for a seat, and here, having unstrapped and mounted her portable easel, she began to make her sketch. There was a drowsy hum about the place, for these were regions of honey bees, and in the delightful solitude her thoughts took their most pleasant way, their central point being none other than the picturesque figure of Grizzly Dick. For two days she had not seen him, for he had gone out on a hunting expedition and had not yet returned. By-and-by the sweet drowsiness of the place overcame her; her hands and eyes relaxed from the intentness of their work, and with a gentle little sigh she slid from the log, and, half reclining against it, slept among the soft grass.

After a while she started, broad awake with that conviction upon her of some new presence, which shows that some of the senses at least guard us even during sleep. She realized that there was some physical stir going on around her, for the log against which she leaned was being shaken, and the sounds, as it was touched, were like sawing and hammering together. Her senses, only half aroused, had still something of the imaginative power of sleep; and even whilst she felt and listened there grew over her some strange feeling of uncanniness. Of one thing she was certain, that her surroundings were not those she was accustomed to, and all awake in a moment her heart began to beat strangely.

> 'As one who on a lonesome road doth walk with fear and dread,
> And having once turned round he turns no more his head,
> Because he knows some frightful fiend doth close behind him
> tread.'[8]

Esse felt herself gasping out the lines as, with instinctive caution, she turned her head round to see what was causing the disturbance.
The sight which met her eyes might well have appalled the

---

[8]   Lines 446-51 of S T Coleridge's 'The Rime of the Ancient Mariner' with some minor misquotation and with Coleridge's lines 446, 448, and 450 run together with lines 447, 449, and 451 respectively in Stoker's three-line version.

bravest. A great grizzly she-bear was tearing a honeycomb from the end of the log, whilst two tiny cubs sat on their haunches by her side. Esse's brain began to throb. She could not think all at once, but her instinct was to remain still, and she obeyed it. Then she began to remember that to feign death is an artifice of the hunter, and she feared lest the bear should turn round, and, seeing her eyes open, would discover her secret, so she shut them close and waited.

But the suspense was awful. Her temples began to throb, and she felt an almost irresistible desire to scream out. Each instant the monster seemed to be coming closer, closer, till its great paw was stretched to tear her heart out, as she had seen it rend the fallen tree to take out the honeycomb. In her fancy she saw the great shaggy head thrust forward, till the big white teeth were close to her, and the enormous mouth was opened to seize her. She could feel the hot breath falling over her, and could even smell the sweet scent of the honeycomb which the bear had been eating ... She could bear the suspense no longer, and opened her eyes. And then a desire to laugh almost as irresistible as that to scream came to her, and instinctively she crammed her pocket-handkerchief into her mouth. The bear was sitting down on her haunches, sucking the honey from her paws, and the two cubs were simply her miniatures in appearance and attitude.

But her mirth was short-lived, for as she looked she saw the bear turn her head suddenly to the opposite side of the thicket and give a low warning growl, which had the effect of drawing the cubs to her side as though they had been attached with springs which had suddenly been released. Between the bear and the edge of the thicket was a low clump of bushes, and to look beyond this she reversed herself on her hind paws, and with a sort of waddle moved to the far side of it. Esse looked on fascinated. As she looked she saw Dick's head rise above the edge of the thicket, and the muzzle of his rifle brought down to cover the bear. He had not seen her, for the clump of bushes and the log hid her easel and herself from him, and his eyes had been so intently fixed on the bear that he had seen nothing else. Esse was afraid to move even an eyelid, lest she should spoil his aim, and waited, waited, with her heart throbbing. Dick meant to take no chances, but just as he was about to fire a slight puff of wind turned the leaves of the sketch-book, which lay on top of the log beside where Esse had been sitting. This was just enough to spoil his aim; the rifle cracked, and seemingly at the very instant the bear, with a wild snarl, threw herself forward at Dick. Esse started to her feet; but the happenings were quicker than her movements. Seeing the bear rushing at him, Dick shifted his rifle to his left hand, and grasping his bowie knife with his right, threw it open with that dexterous jerk which those who use the weapon understand.[9] The bear struck at him, but only hit the rifle, which, driven forward, took Dick on the leg, knocking him off his balance. Esse screamed, but Dick recovered in an instant, and, as the other great paw was raised to strike, drove the knife straight into the beast's heart. But the grizzly bear is a creature of extraordinary vitality, and death seems to reach it but slowly. The uplifted paw fell, and catching him on the thigh, broke it, with the sound of a snapping branch, and threw him down as though he had been struck with a hammer, whilst the forward rush of the great beast took its dead body onward.

It seemed to Esse that all at once Dick lay on the ground, maimed and bleeding, with the great bulk of the dead grizzly pinning him down.

She rushed over to him, and, although the sight of the blood unnerved her for a moment, bent over to help him. Dick lay on his side, with the back of the bear towards his head, and she could see by the way that one of his legs – which stuck out from under the carcase – was twisted, that it must be broken. She seized hold of the bear's leg to try to drag it off, but as she tugged at it unavailingly Dick groaned and spoke to her:

'Hold hard, Little Missy! The varmint has broke my leg, an' is lyin' on it; but don't bother about it yet a minute. We'll have some work to do first! The old gentleman was the one I was followin', an' he ain't fur off. When he sees that I've sliced up his missis he'll come in on the tear, and we've got to look out. Try if you can find my rifle. The b'ar knocked it out of my hand with her first come on, and I fear it's busted!' Esse looked and found the rifle; but it was all

---

[9]   Typically bowie knives were not clasp knives or (in a modern term) switchblades such as the one described here but were sheath knives with a continuous, stationary blade and handle. See Chapter 1, note 10.

destroyed, the stock beaten off, and the barrel bent. Dick groaned.

'Look here, Little Missy, you can't do no good here. You trot off home, and tell Le Maistre to get some of the Indians to come along here with a blanket and a pole. Let them bring their weppins, for if the old gentleman don't get me before they come, we'll get him, sure.'

'Go, and leave you alone!' said Esse indignantly, 'and you wounded and tied down like that? Not me! What do you take me for?'

'By gum! I take you for a plucky little girl, anyhow; an' I shan't never forget it! But what can you do? What can I do, with my weppins gone – for this young lady has got my knife in her, an' is lyin' on it! I can't stir – hold on! What's that?' He raised his hand warningly, and then said in an agonized whisper:

'For God A'mighty's sake, Little Missy, clear out that way!' and he pointed to one side of the clearing; 'and if ever ye clumb a tree in your life, try to do so now! There's the male b'ar on the track. Quick! quick! here he comes!' At that instant there was a fierce growling, the underbush crackled as if violently forced aside, and an enormous grizzly bear plunged into the glade. A grizzly bear is at all times a sight to inspire terror, but when inflamed to do battle he is more than ever appalling. Esse stood a moment paralysed, till she heard Dick's quick shout to her:

'Get out your gun, Little Missy – quick! It's the only chance now!' Esse looked helplessly to where her revolver was hung on the cross arm of her easel; but it was as close to the bear as it was to her, and she knew that before she could reach it the fierce animal, which was even now rearing on its hind legs to plunge, would be down upon her. He had smelled the blood, and had seen the body of his mate, and was full of fury. In her helplessness she had been unconsciously twisting her pocket-handkerchief into a ball in her usual habit, and as the bear dashed forward, she instinctively threw it at him, throwing it in that high, helpless, over-arm fashion which is woman's method. The tiny ball struck him between the eyes, and opening out with the impact, just as a slight puff of wind swept through the glade, for an instant covered his face. He stopped and put up a great paw to tear it down, and as he did so, Esse heard a chuckle from Dick across the glade. This, together with the hiding of the baleful eyes, which seemed to have in some way fascinated her, recalled her to herself; to her dreadful position and Dick's; to the necessity for instant action. With a bound she jumped to the easel and seized her revolver, and as the bear, who had now cleared his eyes, hurled his vast body towards her, she fired once, twice, at random, with only a vague intent of aiming at him, but without marking any special spot. The good fortune which now and again waits on novices seemed to have guided her aim, for one of the baleful eyes seemed on the instant to become obliterated, and then to spout out blood. The grizzly quivered, and, whirling his great paws like the flying sails of a windmill, fell over towards her in a heap. The sharp claws of one of the fore-paws, just grazing her flesh, tore through her dress, and rent it in strips, almost tearing it from her body.

For an instant she gazed at the fallen monster in a sort of stupefaction. From this she was aroused by a wild laugh from Dick; and as she turned to him she saw him slapping the hind quarters of the great carcase of the she-bear as he used to slap his thigh, and heard him say:

'Durn my cats, if Little Missy hain't killed the biggest grizzly on the Pacific Slope with her nose-rag!'

As she looked however, his voice faltered; and as she ran towards him she saw his face grow deadly pale, as flesh does under ether spray,[10] and he sank back seemingly as dead as the mighty brute that lay over him.

---

[10]   Ether spray, ethyl oxide, commonly called sulphuric ether, was sometimes used to induce loss of feeling in an external body part.

FIVE

ESSE rushed wildly over to Dick, and, kneeling down by him, raised his head and laid it on her knee. As she did so she became aware for the first time of the ravages which the bear had made with her clothing, and a hot blush swept over her. In the intensity of her shame it did not trouble her to see that the bear's claws had in that last death-stroke actually cut her flesh, and that her stocking – the remnant of it – was running with blood. She looked despairingly round for a moment in the vague hope of help, but seeing that there was none she braced herself for the superlative efforts which had now to be made. Her reason and even her emotion responded to the call, and she set about her work with a business-like precision. First she felt Dick's heart, and distinguishing its beat, though very faint, knew that he still lived. This made her efforts of feverish intensity, and she worked with an unconscious power and purpose which those who knew her would never have suspected.

First she threw the remnants of her torn dress around her and pinned them together; this was just enough to protect her modesty[1] and did not impede her efforts. Then she set herself to draw the body of the great she-bear from Dick's wounded leg. She knew that it must be taken away in the direction of head to feet so as not to lacerate the flesh with the broken bones or to rub the pieces together. If she could but succeed in removing either the body from him, or him from underneath the body, without further injury to the broken leg, all might be well – at least the smallest amount of harm would be done. So she set herself to examine the situation, and as her eye lit on the bent barrel of the rifle she straightway conceived a plan. She buried one end of it in the ground, close to

---

[1] Esse's 'modesty' here and in the previous paragraph makes her a distinctively decorous 'action' heroine and perhaps provides an illuminating parallel to Mina's odd modesty in *Dracula* regarding her bare feet in the '11 August, 3 am' section of Chapter 8. See *Dracula Unearthed* p155.

Dick's chest, leaving the other sloping up the brute's great side –
this was made with a rough calculation of the weight, so that the
carcase could not topple sideways. Then she got a strong branch
and, using it as a lever, began to try to lift the bear little by little. At
first she could not stir the carcase, but by getting each time the lever
further under she felt at last that it moved. Then, bending her
knees, she put the branch on her shoulder, and, using all her
strength, pushed upwards. The weight rose, and the gun-barrel,
slipping down the side, acted as a strut and prevented it falling
back. With joy Esse looking down saw that Dick's legs were free;
running to his head she took him from behind under the armpits
and dragged him safely away. As it was, there had not been a
moment to lose, for the weight of the bear was slowly sinking the
gun-barrel into the soft ground and a few seconds later the carcase
sank back to its old place. But Dick was free. Then she ran and
filled her cup with water from the little rill that murmured over the
rock in the glade, and raising Dick's head began to try to restore
him to consciousness. It was but the consequence of her womanhood that in the midst of her ministrations she stooped and kissed
the brow, pale under its nut-brown skin, and never thought of
blushing as she did so. The change of posture, and the relief from
the horrible pressure on his wounded leg, seemed to aid in restor-
ing him to consciousness, and after a minute or two of her bathing
his temples, and trying to force a few drops of water into his mouth,
he opened his eyes in a dull, dazed way and looked inquiringly
round him. The first manifestation of instinct was that of the
hunter; that of the man came later. He said in a quick, eager voice:

'The b'ar! Is he dead?' but catching sight of Esse's face a gleam of
fun lit up his own as he said: 'Oh, I remember; you killed him with'
– here he seemed to realize that Esse had not come off scot free in
the encounter, for in a horrified way he said, raising himself on one
elbow, whilst he pointed with the other hand:[2]

'Why, Little Missy, you're wounded. 'Taint very bad, I hope!'

'No! no, Dick – it's nothing. He only tore my dress!'

'So I see. The brute! couldn't he let you alone, anyhow!' Esse

---

[2]   In the climax of *Dracula*, the bowie-toting Quincey Morris also leans on an elbow to
make a speech. See *Dracula Unearthed* p510.

burst out laughing. She had been under such a horrible strain of anxiety and effort that some reaction must come. Dick's remark, and, moreover, the rueful, angry tone of it, afforded the occasion. There was to her something exquisitely humorous in the idea that they too who had just escaped death – if indeed they had escaped, for their troubles were only beginning – should be only troubled about a torn dress. Dick joined in the laugh, but it was rather through his instinct than from any merriness of heart, for presently his laughter suddenly ceased, and with a groan he fell back. He had not fainted as Esse found when she had flown to his side; it was simply that the pain had overcome him, and after giving him some whiskey from his flask he was somewhat restored. But even in his half swooning state he had been thinking, for he now said:

'Wall, Little Missy, guess ye'll have to tramp off by yourself, and send down that help to bring me home. You jest pull my knife outer that b'ar an' find my gun for me if it's lyin' anywheres round, an' put a cup of water by me. Then you jest run off home afore the dark comes on.'

'I'm not going to do anything of the kind! – I'm not going to leave you here alone!'

'Then what in thunder air ye goin' to do? Air you an' me to stick here and have a picnic as long as the b'ar meat holds out? No! Little Missy; ye'll hev to go home, an' soon, or that prospectin' party will have to bring on a bran new coffin for this durned leg of mine!' He winced and almost writhed with pain. In the meantime Esse's mind was made up and she had commenced action. Pulling from the heart of the grizzly Dick's bowie knife, though it made her shudder to touch the bloody hilt, she quickly cut several straight sticks and trimmed them roughly. These she placed beside Dick and quietly began to tear the remnant of her dress, the part which she was not wearing, into long strips; she then filled her cup with water and dipped the bandages in it. Dick looked on with silent admiration, for even in the midst of his pain he could admire her swift dexterity; and with a practical man's instinct, seeing that she was busy with her work, did not distract her, but waited with what patience he could summon. When Esse commenced her efforts to splint the wounded leg Dick helped her, not only with directions, but by shutting his teeth hard and enduring without a groan even her most ignorant efforts. At last the job was done, and Dick spoke again:

'My dear Little Missy, I'm world-wide obliged to ye. Ye saved my life from that old grizzly, and ye've doctored me fine! Now, run off home, an' I'll be all safe here till ye return.'

'I'm not going to leave you, Dick!' she said decisively. 'I'm going to carry you home myself.' Dick laughed feebly, but this time it wounded the girl to the quick; she blushed up hotly, but cooled at once into a paleness, and her answer came with sudden tears into her eyes:

'You wouldn't leave me, Dick, if it was I who was hurt – would you, now?'

'Wall, I should smile!' said Dick.

'Then why should I leave you?' Dick scratched his head; logic and reason failed him as they have failed many a man when arraying them against the strength of a woman's resolve. Besides, Esse had a very forcible argument on her side; in his helpless condition it was utterly impossible that he should oppose any of her wishes. Accordingly, when Esse bent over to lift him, he gave the best aid in his power by throwing his strong arms round her shoulders, and so placing his weight that she could most easily carry him.

And, strange to say, she did carry him all the way home. It is true that the struggle seemed an endless one, and that over and over again she felt that she could have lain down and died of sheer fatigue. But it was for life and death, and to men and women who have true grit[3] great needs give great endeavour. They bring out all that is royal in their natures, from physical strength to highest nerve and psychic power, so that such strength as Nature has manifested to them can be used to the full. Dick suffered a simple martyrdom; for the constant struggle of the weary girl, and her want of usage in such effort, seemed to thrill through the very marrow of his bones, and made the broken leg a veritable torture. But he was a generous and chivalrous soul, and never once in all the long weary hours that followed their outset for home did he utter a groan. Even when, every now and again, the pain overmastered him to such a degree

---

[3]   This American slang term for firmness of character probably derives from the hard particles in the coarse sandstone used for mill- and grindstones.

that he swooned, he did not make any sign, but took his swoon like a gentleman, and sank into it, and awoke from it, without a sign to add to the torture, both mental and physical, which the poor devoted girl, who was struggling on his behalf, endured. Over and over and over again had Esse to set down her burden and rest, her heart panting wildly, and her knees trembling so sorely that she felt that she would be unable even to raise her precious burden again. But each time her spirit rose to the new endeavour, and she attacked the task before her with a fresh energy which surprised herself as much as it did Dick, who helped her loyally to the very best of his power. His heart seemed never to flag or falter, and at times, whilst she sat beside him panting and in almost utter collapse, his ready laugh would ring out to cheer her. She was not even conscious of his swooning, for each time she spoke to him her voice seemed to recall him to waking sense, and he resumed the thread of his own endeavour to cheer her up.

The sun had long set, and the forest paths were dim – like cathedral aisles in the night, when the light through great windows just steals in to show the gloom as an existing thing – when they began to emerge from the depths of the wood and to enter on the steep rise that led to the plateau. Here the moon rose, sailing high in the heavens, and its cheering light gave Esse, now tired almost to unconsciousness, a new lease of strength. With feverish energy she toiled up the steep incline, spurred on by something of the same feeling which quickens the pace of a returning horse, or cheers a spent swimmer who hears the dash of waves on a welcome shore. At the top her arms relaxed, and Dick, now quite unconscious, sank to the ground; and for a little while she lay beside him almost as unconscious as he was.

Suddenly she seemed to wake to the fact that Dick was deathly still, and, forgetting for the moment her own awful tiredness, she sprang to her feet, and, putting her hands to her mouth, sent out a shout for help which rang across the plateau and reached the anxious household, which awaited her with vague apprehension, shared by all, but which none dared to utter.

With answering shouts they all ran out, some bearing lanterns, and came to where she stood beside Dick's body. Her mother screamed when she saw her, for she was indeed but a sorry sight.

The struggle, and the constant forcing a way through undergrowth, had tumbled her hair and thrown it, wild and dishevelled, over her shoulders, and the dust of the forest had grimed her damp face, which also was smeared with blood. The hours of strong effort had kept her own wounds and Dick's open, and from top to toe the white dress in which she had started out – all that was left of it – was smeared, if not drenched, with blood. The flashing lanterns threw into harsh relief the red stains which the falling moonlight[4] had softened, and though the wild picturesqueness of her figure seemed to heighten the effect of her manifest vitality, it could not comfort the heart of her mother, who saw in every item of it danger and pain, and all sorts of unknown possibilities of horror. Recognizing the look in her mother's face, Esse said quickly:

'I am all right, mother. It was the bears, but they are both dead. Look to Dick! he is badly wounded, and I had to carry him home!' and even as she spoke she reeled and would have fallen, only that the strong arms of her old nurse held her up. By this time Le Maistre was kneeling by Dick. Presently he turned round and said:

'He is not dead! I can feel his heart beat! Run for some Indians to carry him to the house!' And without a word, off started Miss Gimp – who up to now had stood wringing her hands – glad of an opportunity to be of some service. Mrs Le Maistre murmured to Mrs Elstree:

'*Some* Indians to carry him, and the dear child carried him all by her poor self up the mountain!'

The Indians were on the spot in a very few minutes, but by this time Dick had recovered his senses, under the stimulant of a little whiskey, and was telling in his own way of the accident and his rescue. At first Esse had tried to put in a word of protest when his praise seemed excessive, but she was by far too exhausted to argue, and Dick's words seemed to have a far-away, pleasing music of their own as he went on:

'I followed the b'ar an' missed him, but see his mate eatin' honey. As I seen her, an' fired, I see Little Missy sittin' beside the log, an' that put out my aim, an' the old lady came jumpin' for me

---

[4]   The combination of white dress, bloodstains, and moonlight prefigures various scenes in *Dracula*.

before I could draw a bead on her. She hit out, and crumpled up my shootin'-iron quicker nor I could see; so I had just time to whip out my bowie, and drive at her before she came at me, an' busted my leg into matches, an' tumbled over me with my knife in her heart, pinning me down everlastingly. Then while Little Missy was tryin' to raise me up the old-man b'ar came whirlin' along; but Little Missy went boldly up to him, and threw her nose-rag in his eye, and while he was clawin' it off, she up with her derringer, and gave it him in the face. He'd just got near enough to rip her tucks out, and scratch her a bit before he went under. Then Little Missy she tackled me like a little hero, as she is, an' dragged the b'ar off my sore leg, an' took an' splinted me up and carried me here like I was a rabbit. Blest, but she's the all-firedest, bravest, kindest, staunchest comrade from the Rockies to the sea! She wouldn't leave me, no, sir! but took me up here all by her little self; an' I'd have died any way, only for her, half-a-dozen different ways – God bless her!' then he said in a whisper to Le Maistre:

'Take me home, quick, old man! I'm racked with pain, and nigh dead, and its torture keepin' it up afore the women folks. I'll be better when I get to my cabin!' Mrs Elstree, who was just bending over, heard the last word, and said:

'You'll go to no cabin, but to my house, and be nursed. I'd like to know what Esse would have done if you hadn't killed the bear; and, whether or no, I wouldn't let you go anywhere else. So that ends it!'

'All right, all right; thank ye much!' said Dick resignedly. 'Ye'll forgive me marm, for my manners, but I ain't pannin' out much[5] in that way just now, owin' to contrairey circumstances!' And so the Indians took him up, and carried him to the house, previous to their going off to the glade, by his emphatic instructions, to get the skins and claws of the two grizzlies, and to bring back the cubs.

For the next few days Esse was obliged to keep her bed, so that she did not know, and was barely in a condition to know, exactly how Dick progressed. The terrible strain, both mental and physical, which she had undergone, brought on a sort of fever; but good

---

[5]   That is, yielding good results, as in finding flakes of gold by placing silt in a pan of water so that the gold in the silt settles to the bottom of the pan.

nursing, and a little antipyrine,[6] finally ousted the fever, and she was allowed to get up. She had of course heard in the interim of Dick's condition, and was anxious to be allowed to assist in the nursing. When she was seated in the balcony, and felt the freshness of the breeze sweeping down from the white summit of Shasta, she had a long talk with her mother on all the events that had passed. First, she learned that Dick was going on as well as could be expected, for his wound was a terrible one, and the hardship of his home-bringing, which she had effected with such nobility of purpose, had much aggravated the original evil. When he had been taken into the house, Le Maistre, who had some little knowledge of surgical dressing, had unbound the bandaging in order to reset it in a more finished manner, but, finding it in good order, waited more skilled assistance. An Indian runner had been sent with a letter to the Doctor at Ashland,[7] and twenty-four hours later he had appeared on the plateau, and had brought to Dick's aid the latest academic skill. When he saw Esse's improvised splint he shook his head, but on his unwinding the bandage, and seeing how well his patient was getting on, he grew enthusiastic on the subject of the mechanical ability displayed in the improvisation. With genuine amazement he learned that it had been effected, under unheard-of conditions, by a young lady who had never seen a broken limb in her life. His wonderment increased when he was told that the slight, pale girl whose pulse he had just felt in the veranda had herself carried the huge bulk of the wounded man up the side of the mountain.

Dick's splendid physique stood him in good stead, and the ruthless stretching of his leg when he was pulled from under the bear, combined with the almost miraculous accident of the rude splints being placed in exact position, had already begun the cure. The Doctor happily prognosticated that within a month, if all went well, Dick would be on the high road to recovery, if not able to move about a little.

'We can never tell,' he said 'what will happen in the way of

---

[6]   Antipyrine is a trademarked crystalline compound derived from coal tar and prescribed for fever, pain, and rheumatism.

[7]   Ashland, in southern Oregon, is about sixty miles north of Mt Shasta.

recovery with a man like that. His simple life, with his great energy and his plain living, make recovery seem extraordinary to town-bred men. But we must not judge of his health and recovery by the standard of the towns, but rather by the animals, who simply lie quiet and lick their wounds, and are running about again when a man is beginning to realize that he is helpless!'

Miss Gimp had been up to this the head-nurse, with Mrs Elstree as a relief; but Esse now joined the nursing staff. Her mother was not altogether satisfied about it, but did not like to make any objection just at present. She was beginning to have an uneasy feeling that perhaps Esse had seen too much of Dick at her impressionable age, though, as yet, she did not imagine that there could be anything serious arising out of their unchecked companionship. But out of her uneasiness came one certain thing – the complete realization that Esse was no longer the child that she had hitherto considered her. She was a woman now, for good or ill; and whatever she thought or did was from the standpoint of a woman, and would have to be adhered to with a woman's constancy, or abandoned with a woman's resolve. Esse had by this time told her mother all the incidents at the killing of the bears, and she could not but see that the circumstance of her own life being saved by Dick – for, with woman's imagination, she realized more than any other episode the agonized waiting till the bear should discover her before Dick came – was an important step in the growth of a romantic affection. She realized as a still stronger one the fact, as Dick repeated to all over and over again, with increasing freedom of speech and added emphasis of delivery, about her saving his life. Mrs Elstree therefore thought that to forbid the girl the sick room would be to beget or increase a desire to see the man, which might develop later into something more serious.

So Esse sat with Dick daily, reading or talking to him whilst he was awake, which was always charming to her; and watching him whilst he slept, which was a much more dangerous pleasure, for then her memory and imagination worked together to weave romances which she durst not think when his eyes were on her, and which were not nearly so real when she was alone. The closed eyelids could not take note of blush or pallor, and had no terror for the maiden spirit in its hour of stress.

Dick was distinctly an interesting invalid. There are men who look their worst under such circumstances, and whose natural petulance under pain or restraint destroys any charm which their weakness may have for the feminine mind; but Dick was not such. There was about him a large-hearted patience and a masculine dominance, on which illness seemed to have no effect. Miss Gimp, who was a born nurse, kept him so clean, and his room so picturesque with summer flowers, that even the memory of his personal carelessness died away from Esse's mind. More than ever the man who had saved her, and whom she had saved, and with whom she had undergone the adventure so sweet to look back upon, became idealized in all those smaller details with which the romantic simulacrum in a woman's mind is in some degree built up. His great amusement at this time was to polish the bears' claws, and to drill them in a particular way, until finally he made a magnificent necklace of them, which he handed over to Esse, telling her that they were fairly hers as she had won them.

When the time of convalescence came, Esse became herself head-nurse. At least, all the labour of amusing the patient seemed to devolve on her. She sat by his side in the veranda reading to him and playing draughts or chess, all of which pastimes were dangerous enough; or often listening to his stories of adventure, which was a thousand times more dangerous. After a while Mrs Elstree came to understand something of the feelings of Brabantio, as he afterwards reflected on the method of Desdemona's wooing by Othello[8] – with the exception that she assured herself that in no way had Dick the smallest intention of making love. Had she known the deeper strata of human passion she would not have so easily thrown aside her fears with a sigh of relief, for the very indifference of the man to the girl's preference, so palpable to the mother's eye, was perhaps the one element remaining to complete the daughter's fascination. Mrs Elstree was, however, a wise woman within her own limitations, and as the summer was drawing to a close she determined not to take any notice at present of what was going on, but to let affairs run

---

[8]   See Shakespeare's *Othello*, Act 1, Scenes 2 and 3. Having learned of Desdemona's marriage to Othello, her father Brabantio is distraught and enraged and supposes that Othello 'hast enchanted her' with 'magic ... foul charms ... [and] drugs or minerals' (1.2.62-74). In *Dracula*, Stoker also refers to Desdemona; see *Dracula Unearthed* p108.

their course till the return to San Francisco. She felt that it would be a less dangerous course than doing anything whilst there was present the opportunity, in the shape of Dick, of matters coming to a head prematurely.

At this time there were two surly people on Shasta: one, Miss Gimp, who seemed never to get farther in her love-making to Dick; and the other, Heap Hungry, whose offerings to the parrot had been cut short by Esse, lest their continuous presence should lead to some awkward revelation.

One morning when Esse looked out of her window she saw the whole plateau white with snow. It was but a tiny dusting of the ground, and had vanished before the sun was high. But it was a warning that the summer had gone, and that Shasta was henceforth to be, for a time, at any rate, but a sweet memory. When departure had been decided upon, all the mother and guardian became awake in Mrs Elstree; day and night she watched, and waited, and bestirred herself so, that there was never an opportunity for Esse to have a sentimental leave-taking. To this end, Dick's natural imperturbability aided, and it was with only a hearty handshake, and a last wave of his cap, that Dick took leave of Esse at the railway station at Edgewood.

Esse herself was too sorry to be very demonstrative. She knew her own secret now, and it took her all her time and effort to so bear herself as to deceive her mother.

SIX

THE change from Shasta to San Francisco for a time altered the course of Esse's thoughts. It was not merely that the atmosphere was different or that the duties of life, in great and little degree, were not the same, but that there were compensations for the loss of the bracing air, the natural exhilaration which is given by a rarefied atmosphere, and the unconventional companionship of Grizzly Dick. There were shops! Shops whose contents were to be investigated thoroughly and their new treasures displayed. There were concerts with divine possibilities, and Esse was a musician cultivated far beyond the opportunities of even San Francisco. Hollander, and Paderewski, and Sarasate were all personal friends of her mother, and from each of them she had friendly counsel.[1] Now that she was come again in touch with all these delightful results of civilization, she began to feel as though the Shoulder of Shasta were barren of the higher delights of life – of some of them at least. Then there were the theatres, for to Esse a theatre was a veritable wonderland. Like all persons of pure imagination, the theatre itself was but a means to an end. She did not think of a play as a play, but as a reality, and so her higher education – the education of the heart, the brain, and the soul – was pursued; and by the sequence of her own emotion and her memory of them, she became, each time she saw a play, to know herself a little better, and so to better know the world and its dwellers. Visits, too, and dances, and the thousand and one harmless frivolities which go to make up a woman's life, claimed her time and her passing interest.[2]

---

[1]   The three musicians named could have been met by the Elstrees in their native city of London (see below in this chapter). Hollander is probably Viktor Hollaender (1866-1940), a German composer and conductor who conducted in London in 1891-97. Ignacy Jan Paderewski (1860-1941), a Polish pianist, performed often in London from 1890 onwards. Pablo de Sarasate (1844-1908), a Spanish violinist, played in London frequently after 1878. In *Personal Reminiscences of Henry Irving* (1906) Stoker indicates that he met the latter two himself in London.

[2]   From a small port town of 858 persons in 1846, San Francisco grew to a city of

And so it was that within a few weeks of return to San Francisco, Grizzly Dick and all his romantic environment became for
the time only a distant memory. But out of this very state of things,
in which her mother had a new sense of security, there came a new
danger. Since Dick was only a memory, he became one with that
particular nimbus of softening effects which is apt to accompany
and environ a memory which is a pleasant one – that which is to a
memory what a halo is to a pictorial saint, at once a distinguishing
trait and an aid to fancy. Esse began to feel that since Dick was a
memory he was one that could be shared; and so each dearest
friend of the hour became in turn the recipient of her confidence.
It is an easy matter to sympathize with a misplaced affection; and
the slaughtering of grizzlies and the saving and being saved by
picturesque hunters, massive of limb and quaint of speech, has a
charm for young ladies unaccustomed to the shedding of blood.
Esse began to hear nothing but praise of Dick, and envious wishes,
sighingly expressed by susceptible companions, that her chance of
love had been theirs. Thus by a subtle process, which the Fates so
thoroughly understood, Esse began to look into her own heart with
the eyes of her friends. What she found there she did not quite
know. All was nebulous, inchoate and dim of outline; but it –
whatever it was – had a living, breathing charm which touched her
imagination, fired afresh all the impulses of her virgin heart, and
made her very nerves tingle at all sweet unknown possibilities.
When a girl gets thus far into the dark forests of love she seems to
realize – historically, but last of all by herself – the truth of that
master of the craft who said that 'a woman loves for the sake of
loving.'[3] There is something in feminine nature which seems to

229,000 by 1890 under the impact of the discovery of gold in California in 1848 and
silver in Nevada in 1859, railroad building, and worldwide exportation of California
wheat. By 1890 the eastern sector of the city, bordering San Francisco Bay, was crowded
with banks, businesses, fashionable stores, lavish hotels, and at least a dozen major
theatres, in which touring European artists regularly performed. Residential
neighbourhoods had spread westward toward the cliffs above the Pacific Ocean, and
palatial mansions of the very rich covered the city's central hilltops. In *The Spectacular
San Franciscans* (1949) Julia Altrocchi characterizes the city's social life in the 1890s –
with its coaching parties, cotillions, and weddings to European aristocrats, for example –
as 'magnificently gay.'

[3]   Probably the 'master' is Lord Byron, who said in the first two lines of *Don Juan*, Canto
3, Stanza 3, 'In her first passion woman loves her lover, / In all the others all she loves is love.'

have a distinct need of expressing itself in some form of self-abnega-
tion. It may be that there is a bacillus of love, which, when once it
finds an entry into the human heart, goes on multiplying itself, as
other microbes do when finding their 'final' destination; or it may
be that it is a virus which can affect all around it in ever-widening
area.[4] But be it what it may, and work how it will, one thing is
certain, that when once this idea has become conscious to a woman
and she can locate its cause, the process of its growth is a natural
one, and nothing in the world can stop it. Thus Esse, having begun
the new phase of her feeling towards Dick by finding in him a sort
of hero of romance, began to exaggerate her own feelings towards
him; and finally grew to believe that she had acted rather badly
towards him.

And here her memory, spurred on thereto by her wishes, began
to play her tricks. She construed in the secrecy of her own soul the
indifference of their parting into a wrong to him; and remorse
began to assail her. She seemed to remember a certain sadness in his
beautiful eyes – for by this time his eyes had become to her memory
beautiful – and to have all the wealth of varied and passionate
expression which is the possession of a young woman's fancy. As
one by one the thousand little incidents of Dick's illness and
convalescence came back to her mind they came accompanied by all
sorts of added charms on his part and small defects on her own,
which fed the fires of her remorse; so that it was not long until as
she sat thinking and recollecting her eyes would fill with unbidden
tears.

This process of Esse's mental unhinging was aided by the care
which her mother took to avoid the subject. She had seen that Esse
had resumed her old life where she had left it, and was rejoiced that
she did so with a physical improvement which she had hardly dared
at the beginning to hope for. Mrs Elstree prided herself on her

---

[4] The 'germ theory' of disease had recently gained wide acceptance and publicity when
Stoker wrote *The Shoulder of Shasta* in the early 1890s. Louis Pasteur, Robert Koch, and
others from the late 1850s onwards had discovered the nature of microorganisms –
'microbes' – and had demonstrated that specific kinds cause specific diseases by a process
in which a pathogenic microbe lodges in a receptive host, feeds from it, thereby creating
toxic residues, and multiplies itself. See, eg, Mary Putnam Jacobs's 'The Discoveries of
Pasteur, Koch, and Others,' in the *Century Illustrated Monthly Magazine*, April 1891, or
Eliza Priestley's 'The Realm of the Microbe' in the *Nineteenth Century*, May 1891.

worldly wisdom, and took special satisfaction to herself that by her patient forbearance at Shasta, she was now enabled to let well alone, without any fear of her attitude, positive or negative, being misunderstood by her daughter. Had she been a more experienced woman, she would not have avoided the subject of Dick, but from her superior position of manifested tolerance could have minimized the effect of his picturesque romance by judicious belittlement. As it was, her silence seemed to Esse a want of appreciation on her part of Dick's heroic qualities; and so it left her daughter to the dangers of her own imagination, with its active and reactive power on memory, and to the less wise sympathies of her girl companions. In the world of Esse's imaginings as to how Dick bore her absence, she began to invest him with a despairing loneliness which became in time but the co-ordinate feeling of her own heart.

Naturally her brooding on this theme, and the secrecy which as naturally became imposed upon her when once she had come to understand its existence, told in time upon her health. She began to grow pale and listless; with poignant fear her mother realized that she was lapsing into her old condition of ill-health – with the added drawback that she had in the meantime passed from girlhood to womanhood, and that her secret tears whose traces she could not always conceal, showed that a new and dangerous emotional side of her nature had been developed. Mrs Elstree thought and thought the matter over patiently, prayerfully, doubtingly, and with a vague, deadly fear which at times became an anguish. She could not conceal from herself that there might be some deep-lying cause in the shape of an unrequited affection, and, naturally she thought that Grizzly Dick might be the object of it. Well, she had known from the observation of her own life and that of the companions of her youth, the truth that was told in Viola's true-false tale:

'She never told her love
But let concealment, like a worm i' the bud,
Feed on her damask cheek.'[5]

---

[5]   See Shakespeare's *Twelfth Night*, 2.4.13-15. Having been shipwrecked in Orsino's dukedom, Viola has fallen in love with him and disguised herself as a male page, Cesario, to be near him; when he asks 'Cesario' about women's love, she describes her own feelings but attributes them to a fictitious sister.

She took counsel with Miss Gimp on the subject, and even asked her opinion as to the possibility of Dick being the object – if indeed, there was one. Under ordinary circumstances the perspicacity of the two elder women who loved her, might have found a way to the knowledge of Esse's secret, and have also found a way for her to its settlement; but Miss Gimp's own feeling for Dick became at once a bar to the knowledge. She had in the discussion her own secret to keep, and this involved a putting aside of the subject altogether. She had also her own end to serve, for she still regarded Dick as a victim to her charms, and a possible object of her settlement in life. In slang phrase she had 'her own axe to grind' in the matter, and looked upon the possibility of Esse's falling in love with Dick as a direct infringement of her own rights. She was only human – and woman – and the stalwartness of her opinion on the subject of Dick set Mrs Elstree's doubts on the subject almost at rest. She determined however to be assured, and took an early opportunity of touching on the subject with Esse herself. She was, however, delicately careful only to touch on the subject in such a manner as not to arouse Esse's suspicions, in case the idea should have no basis in fact, and not to put such an idea in her head, in case it was not fixed there already. And as Esse wished to keep her secret from her mother, who she felt by this time assured would not understand it, it was no wonder that the conversation had the result of clearing all doubts from Mrs Elstree's mind and leaving her under the impression that she had Esse's direct assurance that Dick had no place – and no possible place – in her affections.

The schoolmen doubtless believed when they came to formulate the rules of logic that the *suppressio veri* and the *suggestio falsi*[6] were emanations from the mature intellect of man. Widely they erred! for Eve, the first of women understood them to the full, and it was in that stage of her existence which coincided with a later woman's girlhood that – before she had known Adam and begun to understand the more simple directness of his man's thought and

---

[6]   Schoolmen were writers on logic, metaphysics, and theology who taught in medieval 'schools' – that is, universities. *Suppressio veri* and *suggestio falsi* are Latin terms designating misrepresentation respectively by suppressing a truth and by suggesting that something false is true.

ways – she most fully understood their advantages. Since her time no young woman has ever failed to conceal, by their use, her thoughts on the subject of her affections – when she wished to do so – more efficaciously than a man can conceal his by the direct method of a denial accompanied by blows.

Now and again Esse wore the necklace of bears' claws, for she felt that to omit doing so occasionally would arouse her mother's suspicion; and it was sweet to be able to have so close to her something which was in every way a manifest link between her and Dick. But she continued to grow thinner and paler; and the heart of her mother grew sadder as the time went on.

There came to visit their home in California Street[7] an old friend who occupied a sort of brotherly position towards both mother and daughter. He had been an intimate friend of Esse's father, and on the marriage of the latter had become equally a friend of his young wife. This relationship was not changed even by his own marriage or by Mr Elstree's death, for his wife became, as it were, a partner in the friendly concern, and when Mr Elstree died he left a letter asking him to look after his wife and daughter, and aid them by his help and counsel. He did not burden him with the trusteeship or care of their affairs, for the fortune which he had left to them was sufficiently great to be a care in itself. Peter Blyth was now approaching middle age, and seemed to have gathered to himself in his progress through life all its pleasant possibilities and advantages. He followed, or had followed at some time or other, quite a number of avocations, so that his knowledge was as varied as his taste and sympathy; and as in every phase of his career he had some distinct points of contact with the needs and doings of men he had arrived at a large and tolerant knowledge of human nature. Esse, from her earliest childhood, had known him as a sort of big brother, and had never called him anything but Peter. From him had always come to her something that was pleasant or helpful, from the days that she used to wheedle him into producing the toy

<hr>

[7]   California Street ran (and runs) across the northern part of the San Francisco peninsula from the Bay, on the east side, through the business district, over Nob Hill with its palatial homes, to parkland overlooking the Pacific Ocean at the northwest angle of the peninsula. Since the Elstrees live at Number 437 (see Ch 7), their home would be east of Nob Hill and in or near the business district.

or sweet that she knew was waiting for her in the deep recess of some pocket. When she was in any trouble, either of her own or others' doing, she relied on him confidently to see her through it; and even when she had suffered any childish pain, to hold Peter's hand was a distinct ease and help to her. Naturally between the two had grown up a rare confidence, and up to now in her life Esse had never had a secret which Peter Blyth had not shared. The years that had passed had not aged him in any way, except in the limiting of his physical buoyancy, and in strewing a few white hairs through the thickness of his curly brown beard. This beard of Peter Blyth's was the feature on which a physiognomist would have lingered longest in the setting forth of his character, for it gave a distinctive quality to other features which, though altogether good, were in no wise remarkable. From his beard, and what was all around it, could be deduced the fact that he belonged to the antique rather than the modern world, and distinctly to the pagan school of life. It was not that he was sceptical, for he was not; nor that he was assailed with unconquered doubts, for he had his moods of acquiescence in the fitness of things, and the opposite, as have all men in whose veins the red blood of life flows freely. But there was about him a large-hearted, easy tolerance which made any limited phase of thought a thing rather despicable to him than abhorrent. For all 'isms' he had only contempt, from Calvin to Ibsen;[8] all who held with the ungenerous side of beliefs could not move him from intellectual placidity. His throat had the broad smooth lines which we see in the old busts of Jupiter, and his mouth and chin, which, taken separately, showed the two poles of resolution and of power of enjoyment, pronounced, when taken together, for a conscious *joie de vivre*,[9] which was most certainly not a characteristic of his time.

---

[8]   Calvinism, named after the French religious reformer John Calvin (1509-1564), focusses chiefly on Protestant doctrines of grace, sin, election, and salvation. Ibsenism, based on the plays of the Norwegian dramatist Henrik Ibsen (1828-1906), called for drama that critically and realistically examines modern social conventions; it became highly controversial in England following the staging of his plays in London in the early 1890s and was promoted in *The Quintessence of Ibsenism* (1891) by G B Shaw, who aimed his attack at the kind of romantic, historical, and melodramatic plays staged by Bram Stoker's employer Henry Irving and his Lyceum Theatre.

[9]   French for 'joy of living.'

When he saw Esse his instinct and his knowledge jumped to one conclusion – that there was some secret cause for her low condition, but with characteristic caution he did not betray himself. He then and there determined to take an early opportunity of learning from the girl herself how matters stood. To this end he had a long talk with Mrs Elstree, and in the course of it gathered all the events, great and small, of the life at Shasta. Not content with Mrs Elstree's confidence, he took an opportunity of learning the opinions of Miss Gimp, and thus armed, he felt himself fairly confident of finding out in his talk with Esse the true inwardness of things.

The next morning he came to breakfast with his mind made up as to how he should discuss affairs with Esse. He knew already from her mother all that that dear lady knew, including her put-aside suspicion of an attachment between Esse and Dick, and as he had discovered her mother was manifestly not in Esse's secret, whatever it might be, he knew that there was need for extreme caution. To this end he determined that time should not be of vital importance, for the telling of a secret means on a woman's part a gradual yielding to her own wishes, and a not impossible accompaniment of tears; so he opened the matter with a frank remark:

'You're not looking well, Esse! Too many dances and sittings-out in the conservatory. Suppose you put on your bonnet and come with me for a drive. A whiff of sea air will do us both good.' Esse looked at her mother appealingly, and on her nodding acquiescence, assented joyfully, so Peter Blyth went off to look for a buggy suitable to the occasion. He shortly drove up in a very snappy one, with a pair of horses that looked like 2:40 speed.[10] Esse came to the stoop with a lighter footstep than she had used for many a day, and, her mother noticing it, said to herself, with a sigh of relief, 'The dear child is only tired. She feels already with Peter like her old self.'

As they swept up and down the steep hills that lay between them and the Pacific Peter Blyth tried his best to put and keep Esse in a gay humour. He told her all his best and newest stories, and so

---

[10]   That is, capable of trotting in harness at a speed of one mile in two minutes and forty seconds. In the late nineteenth century a speed of 2:30 per mile enabled a trotting horse in surrey racing to be listed in an official registry as 'Standardbred' in the US, according to John Hervey's *The American Trotter* (1947). The record speed in 1892-94 was 2:04.

interested her with all the little things which had happened in her London home since she had last seen it, that when they came to Sutro Heights[11] Esse was looking more like her old – or, rather, her new – self than she had done since she had parted with Dick at Shasta.

Peter put up his trap at the Cliff House,[12] and having ordered luncheon for a couple of hours later, the two strolled out along the beach to the southward. When they had gone some distance they sat down on a patch of sea grass and looked around them. Below their feet, beyond a narrow strip of yellow sand, was the vast blue of the silent Pacific, its breast scarcely moved by the ripple of a passing breeze. Southwards the headlands, dimly blue and purple, ran out, tier upon tier, into the sea; northwards the mountains towered brown above the Golden Gate.[13] Both were impressed with the full, silent beauty of the scene, and for a time neither spoke. Then Peter, turning to Esse, said:

'What is it, dear, that is troubling you?' Esse started, and a vivid blush swept swiftly over her face, and then left her pale.

'What do you mean?' was her answer, given in a faint voice. For reply Peter took both her hands in his, and said:

'Look here, little girl, that's the first time in all your life that you ever asked me what I meant. Do you really mean, Esse, that you don't understand? Tell me, dear! I only want to help you! Don't you know what I mean?'

Esse's 'yes,' came in a faint voice. Peter went on:

---

[11] Sutro Heights is a natural elevation and large park at the northwest angle of the San Francisco peninsula, overlooking the Pacific Ocean. The property was bought in 1879 and developed by Adolf Sutro (1830-1898) with profits from a vast drainage and ventilation tunnel he had constructed under the Comstock mines in Nevada, according to Doris Muscatine in *Old San Francisco* (1975).

[12] Owned by Adolf Sutro in the 1890s, the Cliff House was at that time a low, mostly flat-roofed structure at the edge of the cliff immediately below the parkland of Sutro Heights and above the Pacific shoreline. Although referred to later in this chapter as a hotel, it appears to have provided only a restaurant and banqueting facilities. According to *San Francisco's Golden Era* (1960) by Lucius Beebe and Charles Clegg, it was notorious for its night-time parties but also was a 'favorite rendezvous for Sunday drivers of stylish rigs.'

[13] The Golden Gate is the strait or inlet one to three miles wide and about three miles long connecting the Pacific Ocean and San Francisco Bay. The well-known Golden Gate Bridge spanning it was not constructed until 1933-37.

'Now that clears the ground. We understand each other. Tell me all about it, Esse! Confession is good for the soul; and I don't think you'll ever find a softer-hearted father confessor than your old friend.'

'Must I tell, Peter?' She spoke in an appealing way, but it was manifest to him that she wished to be treated in such a way that her natural obedience would help her. So he smiled a broad, genial smile, and seeing that her face brightened, he attempted a chastened laugh, and flung some of his good-humoured man-of-the-world philosophy at her:

'Look here, little girl, when we human beings have any secret that's pretty difficult to tell, and that we had rather not tell our mothers, it's generally about the opposite sex. When it's a girl that has to do the telling, well! she's best off when she can get it off her chest to some sympathetic soul that won't give her away. Nature demands that she tells some one, and that some one must be either a friend or the Other Fellow. If it's the Other Fellow then there's no need to tell the friend! But in that case there are rosy cheeks instead of pale ones, and the harmonies of life are set in a full major key instead of the minor. See?' Esse nodded. Peter continued:

'I'll help you all I can, little girl, now and hereafter. Your father was my dearest friend, and one of his last acts was to write to me asking me to look after you and your mother, and to do what I could for you both. If he were here, my dear, you wouldn't need to talk to me! Shut your eyes, little girl, and pretend that he is with you, and open out your heart to him. Don't fear to! Every girl has to, and it is well for them that there are fathers and brothers and friends, to whom they can speak; for otherwise there would be a deal more sorrow in the world even than there is! Esse took his hand in hers and turned away her head, hiding her face with her other hand, and said in a low voice:

'I want to see Dick!' Peter's reply was given with heartiness, although her words sent a mild chill through him. He had almost come to this conclusion already, and he saw trouble – possibly great trouble – ahead for his little friend:

'Grizzly Dick! I've heard all about him, and a mighty fine fellow he must be. No wonder you want to see him, little girl, after all you and he went through together. When your mother was telling me last night about the bears, I was looking at the skins of the two monsters, and thinking that I'd like to shake hands with the fellow that shared that danger with you, and that you were so good to!'

Esse said nothing, but he could tell by the pressure of her fingers on his hand that his words touched her, so he waited a minute or two before going on. Then he asked suddenly:

'Esse, do you want to see him so badly? Is he all the world to you, so that his not being here makes life, with all the good things which it has for you, of no account? Tell me! Speak freely; don't be afraid!' Esse turned her face round, and her eyes were all swimming with unfallen tears. At this moment her heart was full of Dick, and she could look unabashed at Peter whilst she spoke:

'Oh, yes! I want to see him so. The whole world seems so small and cramped without him! If I could only see him for a moment it would be like feeling the wind blowing down from Shasta - like hearing the roar of the falling water - like the sound of the forest coming up at the dawn! It all seems so little here, and he is so brave and strong, and moves through life as though he were born to rule it!' Peter Blyth sat silent, amazed. The young girl's poetic phrases, her full, passionate way of speaking; the very openness of her avowal, were all strange and new to him, and he felt that he must learn more, and then consider well his store of knowledge; so again he asked her:

'Esse, do you think you love him?' She immediately began to cry quietly, and it was only when he had petted and comforted her a little that she was able to reply:

'I don't know! I don't know!' and Peter muttered to himself:

'Hanged if I do, either!' then he went on with his questioning:

'Now, tell me just one thing - I only want your opinion - do you think he loves you?'

'He never told me so.'

'No, but what do you think?' Esse turned to him with all the coquetry of her nature ablaze, and asked:

'What do you think?' Peter Blyth instantly laughed a merry, wholesome laugh which seemed somehow to find an echo in the very recesses of Esse's soul. Somewhere there was hope and comfort for her. This winning trust in a man's power to smooth matters, and the consequent shifting of the burden from her own shoulders was beginning already to work for her recovery. She laughed too, though the laugh smote Peter with pain, for it was like the ghost of her old cheery laugh; but he was glad to hear any approach to merriment, and took advantage of the occasion.

'Come on! Let us get to lunch, and then we shall be able to think better. We *know* now; our next step will be to see what is best to be done, and then to *do* it!' Esse took his outstretched hand, and so, hand-in-hand, they walked by the sea together. Suddenly he stopped and said:

'Look here, little girl, you mustn't go into the hotel with your eyes like that. They'd think that I was the lover, and that I had been quarrelling with you!' He put his hand into his pocket and took out a tiny parcel which he handed to her. Esse took it with curiosity and opened it. Out fluttered a gauzy veil.

'Well, I do declare!' she said, 'I believe this is a put-up job, and that you expected me to cry, and were prepared for it.'

'Of course I did,' said Peter, boldly. 'What else did I come out here for except that you and I might be alone, and that you could tell me your troubles! I knew you would cry! all girls do – under the circumstances!' and he laughed a resonant and ease-giving laugh. So she took his arm and they walked back to the hotel.

SEVEN

WHEN her mother saw Esse, her heart was filled with gladness, for her pallor had given way to a cheerful tinge of rose, and her manner was buoyant and exhilarated. 'Well, I declare,' said she, turning to Peter Blyth, 'an hour or two with you has done her more good than all the doctors in San Francisco in three months. You must take her in hand, and prescribe for her a bit, if you will.' By this time Esse had tripped upstairs to get ready for tea, and Peter, seeing his opportunity, wished to get from Mrs Elstree a comprehensive consent to whatever he might see well to do. All the way home, after lunch, whilst Esse had been chattering to him with all the energy of an emancipated soul, he had been thinking. The problem which he had to solve was a difficult one, and he felt that all his diplomatic acumen would be required. He could not believe that his highly cultured, refined little friend Esse whose fastidiousness, even in her babyhood, had been a little joke in the family, could be really in love with a rough, unmannered trapper. And yet he could not deceive himself that at the present time Esse had an absorbing desire to meet the man; that the unsatisfied desire was sapping her health, and that it would be necessary to take the matter seriously as the only chance of an ultimate solution of the difficulty. It might be that Esse's craving was for the mountain as well as the man; that the place and its possibilities, its adventures, its bracing qualities, the stimulation of the high mountain air and the whole wild, free exuberance which had come into her life at the moment when her womanhood was developing, and as cure for her failing health, had seized on her imagination. In such case, her sense of contrast and the strongly humorous side of her character would be her best protection. In any case, the man was at present so inextricably mixed up in her mind with his surroundings that without his presence no disentanglement could take place. Of course, it might be that when Esse should see him the vague desire for his presence might become an actuality, and that nothing short of marriage with him would content her. If so, then the chance must be taken, for it could not be allowed that her present declining health should not be considered; and if marriage became a necessity, at least Esse had at her disposal all the means of comfort for them both. In a word, the argument ran in his mind: if she should not see Dick she would in all probability fade away and die. If she should see him, one of two things must happen – she would become disenchanted, which was all desirable, or her infatuation would increase until it ended in an undesirable marriage. In any case she must see him.

She must see him – that was certain; and this conclusion having been arrived at, Peter's next point was as to the most advisable way of this accomplishment. There was already experience of the ill effects of her seeing him when his foot was on his native heath. There he was paramount, and his whole personality gathered round itself the romance of the surroundings. If Esse were to see him on Shasta under her present psychic and nervous condition, she would simply tumble head over ears in love with him.[1] There was nothing at all to the contrary; whereas if she were to see him in the midst of her present refined surroundings, she could not help contrasting him with them, with a result that could not altogether tend to further infatuation. Dick therefore must come to San Francisco! Peter felt that his logic was complete, and that no further thought on that part of the subject was required. Thus he had driven up to California Street with his mind so far at rest, and his only present intent that Mrs Elstree should, without even guessing at his knowledge, be content to leave the affair in his hands. So when Esse had gone to her room he turned to Mrs Elstree and said:

'Do you really wish me to prescribe?'

'Most certainly! Look at the effect of your first dose!'

'And you will not blame me if anything should happen that you don't contemplate; or as you should not wish?' Mrs Elstree put both her hands in his and said:

'Peter Blyth whatever you do will be for Esse's good. That is your intention I am sure. I know it; and my dear husband knew it. None

---

[1]   The phrase is a traditional corruption of 'over head and ears' and means 'completely immersed.'

of us are infallible; but you are at least a true friend and a clever man. Do what you will for my dear child's good. Nothing can be worse than to see her fading away from me, as it has been my misery to watch for months past.' She turned away her head, but Peter could see that she was crying as she left the room. When she returned she was cheerful, though there were traces of tears in her eyes. Women have a sort of fixed idea that bathing the eyes with watered eau-de-cologne will remove traces of tears; it is a happy belief, saving much small humiliation, and there are men generous enough to pretend that they are deceived!

After dinner Peter Blyth sat with Esse in the back of the drawing-room, whilst her mother in the music-room opening from it played Liszt and Chopin.[2] His manner was hearty, and his laugh so cheery, that it would have been impossible for Esse to have in his presence been under the domination of any brooding or love-sick fancies, so she fell into the buoyant mood. Now that the strain of keeping her secret was past she felt able to discuss it without doing violence to her feelings. Peter opened the battle with a point-blank shot:

'I have thought all over what you told me, and I have come to a conclusion.' Esse's heart seemed to cease to beat, and she simply listened. 'I think Dick had better come here!' A blush rose under the girl's eyes, and steadily grew, till cheeks and forehead, and ears and neck, were all flushed to a deep crimson. She put her hands before her face but still sat silent. Peter went on:

'I take it, Esse, that this has your approval?' She nodded.

'I take it also that it is your wish?' Again she nodded.

'I take it also that I may – that you wish me to convey to Dick the strong feeling that you have towards him, the keen desire to see him,' – here Esse broke in:

'Oh, Peter, must that be?'

'I fear, my dear, that it will be necessary. He might not be willing to come without such assurance. You see he does not know me at all!'

'But wouldn't it be like my asking him?' Peter laughed cheerfully:

---

[2]   The Hungarian Franz Liszt (1811-1886) and Frederic Chopin (1810-1849) of Poland were pianists and composers.

'It would be uncommonly like it. There is no possible mistake about that! But then the whole thing is uncommon! It is not common that you should care for a man away outside the class you have been reared in; the occasions that threw you together were uncommon. It is uncommon that I should be holding this conversation with you all the time that your mother is playing there in the next room so uncommonly well. I take it also that I had better let Dick know that there may be – later on – a more tender feeling between you? Esse paused. It seemed to her like the probing of a wound this questioning by Peter; and yet it was done with the same matter-of-factness which distinguishes the work of an able surgeon. The wounded have to suffer, and it does not matter if the wound be inflicted by a bullet, or an arrow, or a knife. But there was about the whole thing a sort of business atmosphere, something which tends to suppress romance and to bring into unpleasant prominence the sternest facts; and Esse could not but feel that she was rather following up the logic of the part than expressing her present feelings when she replied from behind her sheltering hands:

'I suppose so!'

'Good!' said Peter. Now I know exactly where I am!' and he rose up to join his hostess in the music-room, whilst Esse lay back amongst the deep cushions of her chair, thinking what a queer place the world is, when even the realization of one's wishes is not a matter of unqualified happiness, and beginning to wonder if Dick would think it strange of her sending such a message. Then she began to wonder how her San Francisco friends with their fastidiousness, their fondness for the ridiculous side of things, and their haughty pride at times, would look on Dick. And then she began to think how Dick would look amongst his new and unaccustomed surroundings. A thousand little traits and habits of his, which she now wished that she had forgotten, recalled themselves to her memory, and she thought it would have been better that she had not told Peter so much, until, at all events, she had some opportunity of seeing that Dick was better schooled to conventional usages. But that could never be until Peter told him! The whole thing was getting so tangled that she could not follow it; and so she stole out of the room, leaving Peter talking to her mother as she played on, and went to bed.

Esse was beginning to feel that an unconventional attachment was not without its drawbacks. The cure was commencing to work!

Next morning, at breakfast, Peter mentioned that he had had a telegram which would compel him to go at once to New York. It might be, that from New York he might have to go on to London; but this was only a possibility, and in any case, his visit home need be only a short one. He would, he expected, be back in San Francisco in a couple of months at the latest. Mrs Elstree was truly sorry that he had to go so soon, but hoped that he would soon be back, and Esse looked at him with a flush and endorsed her mother's sentiments. He received many commissions, and went up to dress for his journey. Before he left he said to both ladies:

'I think I have my commissions all right. Do either of you want to alter anything?' There was no reply, and off he went.

Esse had a half-feeling that she would like to countermand all that she had asked Peter to do, or had acquiesced in his doing. Womanlike, she began to have misgivings when once the bolt had sped,[3] and, womanlike, she felt personally freer now that she had committed herself to a definite act.

Peter Blyth left the eastward train at Sacramento, and took the Portland train on his way north. He had posted himself thoroughly as to the route, and had telegraphed to the station-master at Edgewood to have procured for him horses and a guide to Shasta. On his arrival he found all ready for him, and setting out at once, made good way before stopped by the darkness. Early the next day he arrived at the Shoulder of Shasta, and leaving his guide and horses on the plateau, went at once to Dick's cottage.

All the way up the mountain he had been thinking of the strange job which he had undertaken; and the higher he got, the more the ridiculous side of it came to the front. Here was he, a man of middle age, climbing up an almost desolate snow-clad mountain, to find a hunter who probably couldn't read or write, and to ask him to marry a particularly refined and cultivated young heiress. He had no clue to the man's style, or thought, or ideas, and he could only surmise what his reception might be. Like a good many

---

[3]   That is, once the arrow had taken flight.

Londoners, his sole knowledge of the actuality of Western life was from 'Buffalo Bill' and the 'Wild West Show,'[4] and, from the rough-and-ready energy displayed by some of the participants in these Olympic Games[5] up-to-date, he had strange imaginings as to what his welcome might be like in case he should be regarded as a meddlesome fool – a capacity which, to do him justice, he felt that he filled with quite sufficient satisfactoriness. By the time he had arrived at Dick's cabin he felt not only ridiculous, but in a sort of 'funk,' an unusual thing with him. With somewhat of the feelings of a schoolboy, who learns on calling that the dentist is absent, he found that the cabin door was locked. He had, however, a duty to do, and he did not mean to shirk it, be it never so ridiculous or unpleasant; and so went back to his guide to breakfast.

When he returned to the cabin, an hour later, he found the door unlocked; the owner, however, was absent. He went in and seated himself, awaiting his coming. As he sat, all his unpleasant surmises came back to his mind, and he called himself – inwardly – an unmitigated ass, until the image of Esse's pale face came before him and nerved him. He looked round the cabin, and, as he saw its meagreness and absolute destitution of refinement, he could not

[4]   Named 'Buffalo Bill' while supplying buffalo meat for Union Pacific Railroad workers in 1867-68, William F Cody (1846-1917) gained fame as a marksman and scout in US Army actions against Plains Indians in 1868-72, starred in Western melodramas in theatres throughout the US in 1873-84, organized his own Wild West Show in 1883, and starred in it until 1916, playing throughout North America and Europe, including an immensely successful performance attended by Queen Victoria on May 11, 1887. The Wild West Show was typically an open-air spectacle which began with a parade of scores of American Indians, Mexican vaqueros, and American frontiersmen and cowboys, along with buffaloes and other animals; the show consisted of demonstrations of marksmanship by figures such as Annie Oakley and Cody, riding, lassoing, and Indian dancing interspersed with elaborate skits such as a buffalo hunt, the defeat of an Indian attack on a stagecoach, and, as a finale, an Indian attack upon a settler's cabin or a re-enactment of General Custer's final battle. See, for example, *Buffalo Bill and His Wild West* (1989) by Joseph Rosa and Robin May. Stoker's *Personal Reminiscences of Henry Irving* (1906) and notes from Cody to Stoker in 1887 and 1892 (now at the University of Leeds) indicate that Stoker met and admired him and almost certainly attended the Wild West Show at least twice.

[5]   The ancient Greek Olympics were abolished by the Roman Emperor Theodosius I in 393 AD. Stoker may have been reminded of them by an attempt, discussed in the British press in 1891-95, to create a 'Pan-Britannic' or 'Anglo-Saxon Olympiad' or by the international resolution in November 1894 to create the present-day Olympic Games, which were first held in Greece in April 1896.

bring himself to believe that Esse could really and truly love a man who lived in such a way. The exhilarating air of the mountain, somehow seemed to increase his natural buoyancy of spirits, and he felt that he wanted to laugh, but the gravity of his mission restrained him.

There came a shadow in the doorway and Dick entered, quite unconscious that there was a stranger in his house. When Peter Blyth saw him, the contrast between his appearance and the purpose of his mission was so great that it burst the barriers of his gravity, and the long pent-up laughter broke forth in a flood. He tried to rise, but he was helpless with his paroxysm of cachinnation, and sank back again, and shook whilst Dick looked on in a sequence of emotions. First he was amazed, then somewhat indignant; and, finally, his kindly nature yielded to the humour of the situation, and, throwing back his head, he joined in the laughter till the rafters rang.

There certainly was ground for Peter's laughter when one took in calmly Dick's appearance as the proposee of marriage on the part of a young lady. He had just come back from a hunt of several days' duration, and bore all the signs of hardship and turmoil. Manifestly, he had not washed, even his hands, for several days; his hair was matted and wild looking – unkempt would have been an inadequate word to describe its condition. His clothes were creased with sleeping in them, and were encrusted in places with mud, wherein had stuck bits of twig, dead leaves and pine needles; and from head to foot he was smothered with grease and blood. Killing and skinning big game is not an aesthetic occupation, and is apt to leave just the same traces on the operator as on the artist[6] who wields the knife in a Chicago packing house. In sober truth, he looked like a large, rough, peculiarly dirty, and slovenly butcher on leaving his work. Across his shoulders he carried the skinned carcase of a deer, from which dripped on the floor drops of blood, till they formed a little glittering pool.

Dick, with a hitch of his mighty shoulder, dropped the carcase on the floor, and stood looking admiringly at Peter Blyth, whilst joining in his laugh; then he sat down opposite him on a rough

---

6   That is, butcher.

stool, which he drew towards him by crooking a toe round its leg, and went on with his laugh in greater comfort. Presently Peter began to realize that he was in a more amazingly ridiculous position than that which he had feared, and, with a certain feeling of shame-facedness, felt his laughter die away as he began to gasp out apologies. Dick leaned over, and, lifting a mighty hand, smote the other's thigh as he roared out:

'Durn me, stranger, but ye're welcome. I hain't seen a man laugh so hearty in all my born days, an' I hain't had such a laugh myself since I seen the Two Macs split one another's heads open at the Empire Saloon in Sacramento.[7] My! but I'm glad to see ye, though who the hell ye are, or why ye're here, is more'n I know yet. But we'll know in time. Have ye breakfasted? I'm nearly famished myself; but I've brought in a roast,' he designated it by a kick, 'and we'll soon have a blaze and get fixed right up!' Before Peter could say anything he had strode to the fireplace, and stirring up the embers with his foot, had thrown on them an armful of dried twigs. In a few seconds a fierce blaze was roaring up the rude chimney, and very shortly a chunk of the buck, hung on an iron hook, was already beginning to splutter in the heat. Peter offered to help, but the other waved him back:

'No, sir! This is my shanty, an' ye're my guest! Ye're as welcome in it as the flowers of May. Jest ye sit down and try to get ready another laugh for after breakfast, while I get the fixin's ready. I hope ye can eat saleratus bread;[8] it's all we get up here this time o' year.' As he spoke he was making tea, and setting out his rude table with workmanlike dexterity. Peter could not but admire him as he moved, for notwithstanding his big bulk he was always in perfect poise, and in everything he did he seemed perfect master of it; and he soon lost sight, or at least consciousness, of his dirt and blood, and saw only the splendid specimen of natural manhood, so

---

[7]   For the comedy team, the Two Macs, see Ch 2, note 10. The Empire, like many Western saloons of the late nineteenth century, seems to have included a stage on which variety acts were performed at one end of the barroom. Robert L Brown in *Saloons of the American West* (1978) describes these establishments as more respectable than 'hurdy-gurdies' – that is, bars with a dime-a-dance hall – but nevertheless a combination of 'saloons and burlesque houses.'

[8]   Bread leavened with bicarbonate of potash or with sodium bicarbonate rather than yeast.

magnificently equipped for his wild mountain life and so nobly unconscious of his surroundings.

Peter Blyth felt his feelings mingled; half being of shame that he had so underestimated his host, the other of anxiety as to the future. Matters did not seem of such simple solution as he had imagined. He could not but feel that there was a basis for Esse's unsettlement rather wider than he had thought possible.

When breakfast was ready he sat at table with enjoyment, and, despite want of tablecloth, napkin, or any of the luxuries to which he was accustomed, made a hearty meal. As for Dick he ate to such an extent that Peter had serious misgivings as to whether he might not do himself an injury. When hunger was satisfied Dick took two pipes and handed one of them to Peter with the tobacco canister, and drawing up a rude armchair to one side of the fireplace motioned Peter into it; he took his own seat in a similar one on the other side. Then he commenced the conversation:

'Now, stranger! Wire in,[9] and tell me all about it!' Peter Blyth saw that the difficult part of his task was at hand, and went straight at it:

'I am a friend of Mrs Elstree and of Esse!' Dick rose up and held out a large hand.

'Wall, ye were welcome before, but ef that's yer racket, there ain't no welcome under this ar roof big enough or good enough for ye. Shake!' Then Peter experienced the force of Dick's pump-handle act of friendship; and, like Esse and her mother, felt that Nature might easily have been forgiven if she had gifted her child with a lesser measure of manual power. One good thing, however, was accomplished, the two men were *en rapport*,[10] and Peter's task became more possible. He went on:

'My name is Blyth – Peter Blyth; but no one ever calls me anything but Peter! I hope you will be like the rest!'

'All right, Peter!' said Dick cheerfully. 'Drive along!'

'I saw both the ladies two days ago. Mrs Elstree did not know I was coming here or she would, I am sure, have sent you her very

---

[9]   Literally, send a message by telegraph. Samuel Morse perfected the device in 1844; telegraphic links were established within California in the 1850s and across the US, with the final linkage at Salt Lake City, Utah, in 1861.

[10]   French for 'in touch'; in English usage, 'in a state of mutual trust.'

warm greeting. Esse, however, knew that I was coming, and sent her love.'

'Lor' bless her! Little Missy, I hope she's keepin' peart an' clipper?[11] She kem up here as white as a lily; but me an' Shasta soon set her up, an' she went away like a rose!' Here Peter saw an opportunity of arousing Dick's pity, and at once took advantage of it.

'Poor little girl!' he said, 'I fear she is not at all so well as she should be. She looked pretty pale when I saw her.'

'Do tell! The poor purty Little Missy. I wouldn't see her sick for all the world.'

'I'm sure of that, old fellow! And it would gladden her heart to hear you say that!'

'Well, I should smile! Why, I don't suppose that by this time she remembers there's such a man as me!'

'No, no, Dick – you mustn't think that! Esse thinks more of you than you imagine. Indeed, that's why I'm here now!'

'Why you're here? Say, stranger, you're talking conundrums!' Peter felt the drops gather on his forehead; he was in the thick of it now, and spoke out boldly.

'Look here, Dick, I've come up here on purpose to speak with you! May I speak frankly, as man to man?'

'You bet!'

'And you promise that you will never repeat what I say?' Again the horny hand was held out:

'Shake!' The promise was recorded.

'Dick, that poor little girl is fretting her heart out to see you again!'

'No!' the wonderment ended in a short laugh. 'Go on! What's yer game? Oh, ye're a funny one, ye are!' and he gave his guest a playful push that almost sent him headlong into the fire, whilst his laughter seemed to Peter to hum and buzz amongst the rafters.

---

[11] 'Peart,' as a US term distinct from *pert*, refers to a sprightly good health and liveliness. 'Clipper' is not listed in standard dictionaries as an adjective and is probably a misprint for *chipper*, a US term meaning 'cheerful, lively, in good order.' As a noun 'clipper' was used from the 1840s onwards as a term of praise for a handsome woman and literally designated a trim, speedy type of sailing ship produced first in the 1830s; the derivative adjective, however, was 'clipping.'

Peter went on seriously:

'Honest Indian,[12] Dick! I give you my word of honour that the little girl has been thinking of you till she has nearly broken her heart for want of seeing you. She is as pale as a ghost, and her poor mother has been fretting her life out about her. Now, won't you do something for her?'

'Do somethin'! Why look here! ye may take the full of her purty little body of blood out of my veins for her, if that will do her any good!' This time it was Peter Blyth who held out his hand, and said: 'Shake!' Then he went on:

'You know, Dick – or perhaps you don't know, living up here all alone – that young girls have strange fancies, and their affections don't always go where their elders would like to see them. Esse has been a good deal with you, they tell me, all last summer; and after all, you're a man! By George, you are all that! And she's a woman! And it seems to me – you understand, old man! Why need I go on!' A blush, a distinct and veritable blush, as pronounced as might be found in any ladies' seminary in San Francisco suffused Dick's face, and he turned away with a little simper that would not have disgraced a schoolgirl. 'Why, ye don't mean to say,' he went on sheepishly, 'that that purty thing wants me for her bo?'[13] His bashfulness kept him silent, and Peter Blyth looked on in fresh wonderment to see such awkward modesty so manifestly displayed in the person of such a blood-stained ruffian as he looked. Dick's embarrassment, however, was only momentary, and ended, as did most of his emotions, in a peal of laughter. Peter looked on with qualified amusement; it would have been all pure fun to him only for the memory of Esse's pale face in the background. Dick suddenly stopped and said:

'What do ye want me to do?'

'That's right, old chap! I want you to find your way down to San Francisco, and let Esse get a glimpse of you. It will bring back to her all this beautiful mountain, and she'll feel the wind from the snow peak blowing once more on her, if I know her!'

---

[12]   An American colloquialism coined at least as early as 1851 meaning 'honestly' with emphasis. Stoker repeats the expression in *Dracula*; see *Dracula Unearthed* p315.
[13]   Beau.

'Good, I'll come! It can't be for a few weeks yet, for I have undertaken a contract that I must get through with; but I'll come. That's cert!^{14} Where does she live in 'Frisco?'

'In California Street, No 437, the big house with the stone seals on the steps. Dick, you're a brick! Old man, you'll be very tender with her, will you not? Remember it was a great struggle to her to let me gather even so much of her wishes as I did. She's only a young girl; and you must make things easy for her! Won't you? Don't shame her by making any overture come from her?'

'Say, what's that? Over what?'

'Overture! It means, old man, that you mustn't leave it to her to do the love-making, if there's any to be done.'

'Hold hard there, pard! Easy up the hill! I ain't much of a feller I know, an' my breedin' has been pretty rough; but I ain't such a fool as to leave no girl to do the courtin' when I'm on the racket!^{15} Ye make yer mind easy! – Say, must ye go?' for Peter had risen.

'Yes, Dick, I'm bound to be in New York without a day's delay. I've important business awaiting me there; and say, Dick, if things don't turn out as I think, and as you may think too, when you see her, you'll make it easy for her, won't you?' Dick looked a perfect giant as he stood in the doorway following out his guest, for all the manhood of him seemed to swell within him, and to glorify him till the blood and dirt on him seemed as if Viking adjuncts to his mighty personality. His words came deep and resonant as from one who meant them:

'Look you here, pard! That dear little lady is the truest and bravest comrade that ever a man had! She stayed by me in the forest, when it was good time for her to go, with the biggest grizzly on the California slope comin' up express. She fou't him, for me, an' killed him. An' then she wouldn't leave me, even to get help; but she carried me alone, although she was wounded herself, more'n a mile up the mountain side! She took me outen the grave and hell and the devil, an' I ain't goin' to go back on her, so help me God! I don't want to be no trouble to her, nor no sorrow, an' I think it's a mistake of her choosin' such a man as me – but I tell ye

---

this: She'll do with me what she likes, an' how she likes, an' when
she likes, an' whar she likes! The wind doesn't blow that's a-goin' to
blow between her and me, if she wants me by her side!'

EIGHT

WHEN Esse found that there was a possibility of her again seeing Dick she began to become reconciled to the existing condition of things. It was true that as yet she had only a glimmer of hope, for Peter Blyth had not been explicit as to his intentions. In the first place he might not be able to find Dick, for his journey to New York, and possibly to Europe, might eventuate in complications which would forbid his returning to California at all; in any event for a long time. Then again, Dick might not see his way to come to live in cities, and Esse had already begun to appreciate the refinements of life sufficiently well to make it impossible for her to even contemplate an isolated life in the woods or on the mountains. Picnicing, and especially in a honeymoon form, might be delightful, fascinating, of unspeakable joy; but such life, without relief, would never suit her as an unvarying constancy. From the glimpses which she had had into Dick's shanty she knew well enough that the measure of his refinement would not reach her own minimum standard, and she had doubts from her experience of his improvement in small matters if he would readily lend himself – if he could lend himself, even if he so desired – to a loftier social condition. These were certainly arguments which tended to damp the zeal begotten of absence, and the stimulating effect of pleasant memory working upon a morbid but fervid imagination. When in the anæmic condition Esse's imagination was apt to run away with her, though when her system was well furnished with red blood her fancies and desires were healthy and under control. Now that the strain of her self-imposed secrecy had been relieved, her health began to mend, and the improvement was manifest in the ready manner in which she yielded herself to her surroundings, and began to make the most of them; thus mental and physical health began to act and react on each other, and Mrs Elstree's heart rejoiced as she saw the improvement in her daughter. Soon Esse began to show something of the same robustness which she had achieved on Shasta. Her chalky pallor yielded to a delicate rose colour which, tingeing her brown skin, made a charming union of health and refinement. Her figure began to fill out, and within a few weeks from the time of Peter Blyth's departure she looked quite a different being from the pallid, meagre, green-sick[1] girl whom he had left. Peter had telegraphed from New York that he had to go to London, but that he looked to return in about two months. He had said nothing of Dick, thinking it wiser to be silent until he knew for certain whether he would turn up in San Francisco. Mrs Elstree did her best to keep Esse up to the mark of health and energy at which she had arrived; and she so laid herself out to this end that her house became the very centre of the most pleasant circle in San Francisco. Every stranger who arrived was of course introduced to her, and not a few found an excuse for prolonging their stay in order to share again her charming hospitality and the companionship of Esse. There was a constant succession of luncheons, dinners, balls, picnics, and all those harmless gatherings which have no definite name, but which have a charm of their own in their freedom and the relaxing of the bonds of conventionality.

Amongst the strangers who came, and in natural course made Mrs Elstree's acquaintance, was a young English painter, who had already made a great name for himself. He was one of those who had not attached himself to any art school long enough to be cramped by its inevitable littleness. He had skipped lightly through the various schools of the world, learning and adapting all their methods to his own genius, and keeping his mind and imagination fresh by a perpetual study of Nature in all her moods. Partly by nature, and partly by merit of his varied training, he was of a most charming personality, with gentler manners and keener refinement than might have been expected from his strength and stature. As, in addition to his other qualifications, he was remarkably handsome, it was small wonder that he was looked upon with favour by the ladies in San Francisco, and with a certain reserved tolerance by the men. Even the instantaneous heartiness of his reception by the Bohemian

---

[1]   Green-sickness, or chlorosis, is an anæmic condition caused by iron and protein deficiencies; it afflicts young women most frequently and causes a greenish pallor of skin.

Club[2] did not allay the misgivings of certain young men of pleasure, unattached.

Between Mr Hampden and Esse a friendship soon sprang up, and this was fostered by the opportunities given by her sitting to him for her portrait, and his finally coming to stay as a guest in the house. To him the freshness and artless simplicity of Esse was akin to those grand simplicities of Nature which had been the study of his life; and it was little wonder that when for some time his art and human sympathies had been thus united and centred in so charming a young lady as Esse, his feelings of friendship should have taken a warmer turn. Before the month was over he was head over ears in love with her.

And Esse? By this time, sad to tell, Esse had quite overlooked, if indeed she had not forgotten, the fact of Dick's existence. Sometimes, when some accidental allusion or expression suggested the idea, she remembered him, but as a far-off and independent fact; she never connected him now with her own life. He was, and would be till the end of her life, a true and faithful friend, whose memory was set in a frame of romantic picturesqueness, as a miniature is set round with diamonds; but he did not belong to the living present at all. And, strangely enough, when he had come to occupy this place in Esse's mind, all the pleasant things began to cluster round him again. His individuality was a centre round which crystallized all the pleasant lesser memories of the summer on Shasta. Once or twice in the night time, when something kept her awake, Esse thought, with burning blushes, of her confiding to Peter Blyth the one secret of her life. She wondered how she could have done such a thing, and was angry with herself for what she now considered her mistaken idea as to her own feelings, as well as for her unmaidenly confidence. With a gush of thankfulness she

---

[2]   Located at Grant Avenue and Post Street in the 1890s, the Bohemian Club was organized in the early 1870s by writers and artists and soon became an elite club dominated by a much broader, more conservative membership. The club remained dedicated to the arts, however, and to lively gatherings fittingly called 'High Jinks,' according to Doris Muscatine's *Old San Francisco* (1975). During Bram Stoker's visit to San Francisco in September 1893 with the Lyceum Theatre Company, his employer Henry Irving 'underwent the hilarious experience of being initiated into ... the Bohemian Club' at a lavish dinner which is described in Austin Brereton's 1908 biography of Irving.

remembered Peter's sudden call to the East, and determined that on his return, and before any harm could be done, she would set *that* matter right in a few words. Mrs Elstree saw what Esse herself did not see, that she was herself becoming, nay, had already become, in love with the young painter; and as she in every way approved of him as a possible son-in-law, she allowed matters to freely run their course. Esse's romantic feeling for Dick belonged to the school-girl phase of her existence; but the new affection was the expression of her woman's life, and it differed as much from the former in its strength as in its consciousness. The episode of Shasta was, in a sort of way, the 'preliminary canter' of her affections, and had all the consciousness of its limited purpose; whereas the later and truer love had all the unconscious, serious earnestness of the race itself, where means are forgotten and only the end is held in view. There was no thought of Dick in her mind, no regret, no remorse, even no pity of his wasted and ruined life, as a few months ago she would have considered it. There was, in fact, no thought or recollection of Dick at all, when, in answer to Reginald Hampden's passionate appeal, she put her two hands in his, and their lips met in love's first long kiss.

That evening, as they sat hand-in-hand in the little drawing-room, where there was no one else, in that early darkness which is the nearest thing to twilight which California can produce, Esse, with a manifest purpose, and with many flutterings of the heart, told Reginald that she had a confession to make. He, with the amused, superior tolerance of a successful lover, encouraged her by gentle words and manifold tender caresses to proceed. As a man of the world he knew that, as a rule, the sins which well-bred young ladies have to confess to their *fiancés* are merely self-distrustful exaggerations of minor indiscretions, or breaches of temper. With a sinking heart Esse began, for now that she had to speak of Dick again to a third person, his figure loomed up uncommonly large into the foreground of her thoughts.

'It is about Shasta!' she said, in an almost inaudible voice.

'About Shasta, dear, that is lovely! I like to hear you speak of that sweet spot! I think I am in love with it myself from what I have heard you and your mother say of it. I am thinking already, Esse' – here he drew her closer to him – 'how you and I shall go there some

summer and have a fresh honeymoon!' Esse was silent; there were
conflicting thoughts in her mind, and she listened as he went on:

'You shall show me all over the place; the seat on the rocks on
the edge of the plateau, where we shall see together the sunset over
the sea; the sun-dial of the trees by which we shall reckon the hours
of our happiness – for, my dear, we shall not be able to keep any
other reckoning, they shall go so quickly; the spot where you killed
the bear; and then we shall come up the way you carried Dick. You
see, dear, I know them all!'

'It is about Dick I want to speak!'

'Speak on, Esse dear; I like to hear about him! What a splendid
fellow he must be! I want to shake him by the hand; he saved the
life of my little girl, and she saved his! Why, we must be like
brother and sister to Dick!'

'But, Reginald, I must tell you about him before you say –' Here
Reginald interrupted her.

'Isn't Dick the splendid, brave fellow that I think him; the
manly, upright gentleman of nature, with the freshness and
splendour of the wood and mountain upon him!'

'Oh yes! he is all that; there is nobody in the world braver or
nobler than Dick! You can't say anything too good of him. But
that's just it! You may not like it that I – one time – before I met
you – thought all the world of him!' Reginald laughed, and caught
her again to him; he was glad of these excuses for demonstrative
affection.

'Oh you dear little high-minded goose!' he said. 'Why, of course
you thought all the world of him! So would any girl! If I were a girl
I would go my boots[3] on a splendid fellow like that.' Esse began to
breathe more freely, though the worst was yet to come; she had to
finish her confession. She bravely went on:

'That would be bad enough if only you knew it, but I told it to
Peter Blyth!'

'And who may Peter Blyth be?' asked Reginald, with a tinge of
jealousy in his voice.

'He is an old friend of my mother's. He was my dead father's
greatest friend, and he is a sort of guardian to us both.'

---

[3]   That is, he would wager or bet his boots.

'Oh!' said Reginald, partly satisfied, so Esse went on.

'I don't know why I told him – that I – I – wanted to see Dick – but I did; and he said he would see Dick some time and that he would come and see me!' Here she covered her face with her hands, and in the dusk Reginald could see that she was crying. He took it that it was partly from regret and partly from vexation, so he asked another question in order to distract her mind:

'And did he come?'

'Oh no!' Esse started up and looked at him with wet eyes. 'Oh no! and I hope he never will! Peter Blyth was called away to New York the very next day, and from there had to go on to London, so I am in hopes that he will never tell Dick. When he comes I shall ask him never to say another word about it again as long as he lives, or never even to think of it!' Reginald thought for a moment and then spoke. 'Would it not be well to send Mr Blyth a cable?'

'Why so?'

'Because he might go up to Shasta on his way back. And, my dearest, that would never do. In addition to making you uncomfortable it would not be fair to Dick. He would take it to heart that he had been so invited; and without any blame on his part he would feel that he had been deprived of a great happiness!'

'Oh, Dick would not mind!'

'How do you know?'

'If he had cared about me he would have said so long ago!' from which it could be seen that poor Dick's silence was already beginning to be construed into a fault, and his blindness into an offence. Reginald hardly took the same view as Esse on the subject, but he was none the less contented. However, they agreed that it would be no harm to send a cable to Peter Blyth to his London address, for Esse did not know where he stayed in New York, and the following was despatched:

'Do nothing about Dick till I see you. – ESSE.'

The next evening Mrs Elstree had a reception of all her friends, and she thought that it would be a good occasion to make known Esse's engagement. Her receptions were given in English style, and as she had brought over English servants, her Californian friends were always interested in the way things were done. They generally ended however in an impromptu dance, American fashion. When the night arrived Mrs Elstree received, just as she was going to dress, a telegram from Peter Blyth:

'Arrive in evening; dining on car.' So she gave instructions to have his room prepared. Presently the guests began to assemble, and both Esse and her mother were busy receiving them, Reginald naturally not being far off, and being now and then introduced in his new capacity. There were congratulations on all sides, and a well-bred hum arose throughout the rooms.

In the midst of the festivities a tall, powerful-looking man, walking with long strides, but putting his feet down as though they were cramped, came to the house and knocked. When the liveried footman opened the door he said:

'Say, boss, does Mrs Elstree live here?' The man had only been imported a few days, and, as he had come to the West with vague ideas as to snakes and scalping, and other American common-places, and would not have been surprised if he had seen a tribe of Indians on the war-path in Montgomery Street,[4] answered with his usual imperturbability:

'Yes, sir, she receives to-night.'

'Kin I go in?'

'Certingly, sir, if my mistress was expecting of you.'

'I know Little Missy is.'

'Miss Elstree is within too, she receives with her mother.'

'Then, General, I guess I'll just cavort in and pay my respects.' The man motioned him in, and he was handed over to another footman, who took his hat and said:

'What neem, sir?'

'Guess, Colonel, you have me there!'

'What neem shall I enounce ?'

'My name? Oh, I tumble![5] Jest you say Grizzly Dick of Shasta!' The man called up the staircase to another footman half way up:

'Mis-tar Greezly Dick of Shost-ar!' The second man called on to another, at the door of the drawing-room:

---

[4]   Montgomery Street runs north and south in eastern San Francisco through what was the heart of the business district in the 1890s and crosses California Street near the site of the Elstree home on that street in the novel.

[5]   Here 'tumble' is used in an unusual (but not unheard of) figurative sense of tumbling upon something and means 'understand something not clearly expressed.'

'Mr Greazy Dick of Shostar!' And the latter shouted the name into the room, in a Hibernian accent:[6]

'Misther Crazy Dick Shostoo!' Dick was for an instant amazed by the wilderness of strange faces, the myriad lights, the hum and movement of the scene; and as for Mrs Elstree and Esse, they were for a moment ignorant of the personality of their visitor. The Dick who now stood blinking in the doorway, and awkwardly shuffling his feet, had little resemblance, except in stature, to the Dick whom they had known on Shasta.

When the time for his visit to San Francisco was ripe, Dick had come as far as Sacramento, and had then prepared himself for what he considered a fashionable visit. This he did by getting himself up as like as he could to the more aristocratic-looking of the Two Macs, as that individual had dwelt in his memory, combined with the most stylish of gamblers and barmen, from living examples. His general effect was enhanced by the failure of the goods exhibited in the various tailors' shops, and 'misfit parlors' to adapt themselves to the great bulk and free, sinuous carriage of the hunter. Dick had thus arrayed himself in a blue claw-hammer coat with brass buttons, a low-cut waistcoat of mighty pattern,[7] in plaid of many colours, in which primary shades of scarlet, yellow, and blue, predominated, a light pair of yellow cord trousers, of preternatural tightness, and enormous patent leather pumps, which were all too small to be easy on feet accustomed to mocassins. His shirt was what far-western salesmen call 'dressy,' and exhibited on its bosom many rows of fancy pleating with, between them, masses of herring-bone hand-work, such as the rustic maiden is wont to exhibit on her Sunday petticoat. A red tie with big bows and fringed ends, and some massive gold studs of fancy pattern, to match the watch chain, which lay across his diaphragm like a hawser, completed his toilet. But Dick, not feeling complete, even in this subjugatory attire, had been to the barber's and undergone a process of curling, oiling, and scenting, which alone would have isolated him in any high-bred society throughout the world. Add to these disadvantages a manner

---

[6]   That is, Irish accent.

[7]   A claw-hammer coat is a tail-coat for evening dress; a waistcoat is worn under an outer coat (originally under a Renaissance doublet) and is often chiefly ornamental and meant to be seen.

composed of equal parts of unchastened ease of gait and shy awkwardness, and it is little wonder that the ladies did not at once recognize their old friend the free-gaited, bold, natural child of the mountains. Esse was the first to recognize him, and stepping forward, held out both her hands with eager welcome, utterly forgetting, in the surprise of seeing him, her previous anxiety as to his possible coming. At the moment, however, Dick had recognized Mrs Elstree and had stepped forward and taken her by the hand, and was beginning to work the pump-handle shake, which she already knew, and dreaded. This peculiar shake of Dick's was a work of time, and Mrs Elstree knew that the best way to get over it was to submit quietly; she was not sorry also, to have a moment in which to collect her thoughts, for it flashed on her that so strange an appearance, and so unexpected a coming, must have some special cause. She had a half fear that there was some trouble in store for Esse, or with her; and as she knew that the eyes of all fashionable San Francisco were on her, she felt that it behoved her to be cautious. She instantly determined on a course of action – heartiness. Dick was an unconventional person, and when the guests knew and realized who and what he was, the manifest surprise and amazement with which they were already regarding him would cease. He had saved Esse's life, and she had saved his, and under very strange and unusual circumstances. This alone would justify his appearance, and any reception that might be accorded to him. So she said effusively:

'Why, Mr Grizzly Dick, this is a treat! I am delighted to see you in San Francisco! Do you make a long stay?'

In the meantime Esse stood with outstretched hands, for she did not like to draw them back, lest Dick should think she was offended, and so waited. Before Dick could reply to her mother he saw them, and answering: 'Thank ye, marm!' turned to Esse and said:

'Wall, Little Missy, if this ain't jest the all-firedest, highest old time as ever was. My! but ye look purty; like a ripe apple ready to be bit. An' do ye remember the b'ar, and the way yer frock was tore all away? Durn me if the old-man grizzly was here himself now, he wouldn't have the heart to lay a claw on ye!' As he spoke he had taken her hand, and was subjecting her in turn to the pump-handle ordeal. Esse answered with what heartiness she could muster, for there was a look in Dick's eye, a sort of assuring her, which was quite new to her, and which made her anxious as to what might happen. She would have given worlds that her mother knew the exact state of affairs, for she could and would have helped her at any cost; but her mother did not know, and she must now trust to Providence and the chapter of accidents. In the meantime, other guests were arriving, and they both had to receive them. Mrs Elstree saw so much of the difficulty as that Dick would become a nuisance if he did not pass on with the rest, so she said sweetly:

'Won't you take a seat for a few minutes, Mr Dick? Esse and I have to stand here a little while to receive our guests; but we shall come to you very soon.' Dick laughed his boisterous laugh – how Esse felt at the moment that she disliked it – which more than ever attracted all eyes to him, and with a rough bow and a 'Count on me, marm, every time!' withdrew to the other end of the room. Feeling thoroughly awkward in such a novel situation, he began to make up for his want of *savoir faire*[8] by brazen impudence, this being his idea of easy deportment.

At this time, Peter Blyth arrived at the house, and went upstairs to his room to dress himself for the evening.

---

[8]   French for 'knowing how to do,' referring especially to a polished sureness in social behaviour.

NINE

I T was some little time before either Mrs Elstree or Esse could get an opportunity of rejoining Dick. The news of Esse's engagement had got about, and all her friends made a point of coming round to offer good wishes. The stream seemed to Esse as if it would never end, for with each moment her anxiety grew. Those who have not experienced it cannot understand the rapidity with which a desire for a few moments' thought grows, until it becomes a sort of agony. Esse was in a way chained to the social stake. She had to stay by her mother, to smile, and give her whole thoughts to what was going on around her. She would have given anything to have had time to warn her mother, or Reginald, to take care of Dick, and find out his purpose; for all the time unconscious cerebration[1] was working, and she was rapidly coming to the conclusion that Peter Blyth's message had gone, and that Dick's presence was an answer to it. Reginald saw with the eyes of love her anxiety, but could do nothing to allay it; he, too, was chained to the stake by the exceptional circumstances of his social duty. Presently they heard a loud laugh in the room behind them, followed by a titter of feminine voices, and a louder laugh from men. Esse felt her ears burning. Her mother shot a quick glance at her and said *sotto voce*:[2]

---

[1]   'Unconscious cerebration,' according to Robert J Campbell's *Psychiatric Dictionary* (1981), is a now-obsolete term meaning 'mental activity without conscious direction.' The Oxford English Dictionary ascribes the first use of the term to Dr William B Carpenter in *Principles of Human Physiology* (4th ed, 1853). The term appears twice in Bram Stoker's *Dracula* (1897) and helps to create one strand of explanation for Lucy Westenra's and, by implication, Mina Harker's vampirism in terms of the late-nineteenth-century psychological concept of 'double' or 'dual consciousness' (see, for example, *Dictionary of Psychological Medicine*, 1892, edited by D M Tuke). In *Dracula's* Chapters 6 and 20, Dr Seward refers to his own thinking and that of his patient Renfield as 'unconscious cerebration'; this parallels and amplifies Dr Van Helsing's diagnosis of Lucy's alternating normality when awake and vampirism when sleepwalking or in a trance as 'dual life' in Chapter 15. See *Dracula Unearthed* pp124, 292, 371-72.

[2]   Italian for 'under the voice'; in English usage, 'softly, in an undertone.'

'Never mind, dear, we shall be able to attend to him in a few moments; I see the stream is slackening.' A few minutes more and the last of the guests, except stragglers, had arrived, and they were free to move about. Esse went off to look for Dick, for she felt that he was safest with her, and that she was safest too, for she did not know what he might not do or say in his strange surroundings. She found him in the midst of a group of the smartest young people in San Francisco society. Poor Dick in his ignorance thought he was getting on capitally, for in the society in which he had hitherto mixed the person who caused the loudest laughter was most esteemed of the company. He had with his native taste and daring selected out the prettiest girl in the room, one who though ostensibly one of Esse's 'dearest friends' yet bore her no good will since it had been apparent to her that Reginald Hampden, upon whom she had set her heart, was in love with her friend. The recent knowledge of their engagement was gall and wormwood to her, and she was delighted to have an opportunity of making Esse feel uncomfortable. Dick had opened his conversation with a piece of complimentary pleasantry such as he would have used to a barmaid in a dancing saloon, nothing coarse, nothing unpleasant, but altogether familiar and out of place in a conventional assembly. The young lady was not offended, a girl very seldom is at being singled out for compliment by a fine-looking man, be he never so rude in his style; but she saw her opportunity, and led him on. She had seen the familiarity of Esse's greeting, and, though she did not comprehend the whole situation, saw that there was fun for her and others, and some sort of humiliation for her friend. So she at once began to ask Dick questions, and to encourage him to laugh and make remarks. Some of her smart set came round, and a game of refined bantering began, the victim being unconscious of his ridiculous position, and of the ridicule showered upon him. That was the fun of the game – Dick was not the build of person that a man would ostensibly make game of, unless he wanted a fight. She asked him all about Esse, and supposed all manner of things as to their friendship; and in fine brought Dick to the point of bragging, not of his own prowess, but of hers. This involved an appearance of familiarity with Esse, and as he went on she gently insinuated that they must be great friends: at last she daringly said:

'If I was a man, and a girl saved my life, I would ask her to marry me. I think it would be the least I could do!'

'Now, do ye really think so, miss? Wall, I do admire! Do tell, now, how ye'd set about it?' Poor Dick had quite fallen into the trap through his very simplicity, and the honesty of his purpose in coming to the city. His tormentor, gathering courage from the winks and smiles of her male admirers round her, said:

'In the most open way I could! I'd ask her before all her friends, so that there might be no mistake. If I wanted to honour her by the offer of my hand and heart there should not be any slouch about it!'

'Shake!' said Dick, extending his mighty hand, and half a moment later his new friend, with a rueful smile, raised a crumpled hand, and looked at the blood, where her rings had cut into her crushed fingers, which was beginning to show through the rent in her glove.

'Oh, I say,' said one of her admirers, 'has the clumsy brute hurt you?'

'Miss,' said Dick, 'I humbly beg yer pardon! I never thought of how tender ye women critters is. I should have known better.' Then he turned to the last speaker and said:

'Look here, Jedge, I wouldn't be so free with them cuss words o' yourn. Ef ye fling them about so promiscous, some one is apt to be hurt. They're worse'n chunks of rock, anyway!' The man addressed ran his eye up him from his boots to his oily hair but said nothing.

At this moment Esse came forward, and Dick, seeing her, and with her a way out of the embarrassment due to his clumsy strength, stepped towards her, and delivered himself of a little speech which he had rehearsed to himself an innumerable number of times on his journey from Shasta. He had submitted it to his casual friends the bar-keeper and the barber at Sacramento, and armed with their approval, and fortified by the expression of Esse's young lady friend, whom he took to typify fashionable society, and who had used almost his words, he had no hesitation now in speaking. Dick was in no wise a coward; he could face an awkward situation, and, like many another man, he had only to begin to find all his difficulty removed. Esse stood amazed when he began his speech, and for a moment looked helplessly round her; but then, catching Reginald's eye as he stood on the outskirts of the little throng, braced herself to the situation, and smoothed her face to a grave smile by mere force of education and habit.

'Little Missy! An honest man's love is all that he can give the proudest lady! I am only a simple man, but I have come from the snows of Shasta to do ye the only honour in my power. I am glad to do it before your honoured friends and your family circle. Will you honour me by becoming my wife and giving me your heart and hand?' Having spoken, he looked calmly around him, as one does who has done a meritorious action, and done it well. Esse felt the blood rushing up to her head, and burning her cheeks and ears, as she heard the titter of laughter around her. Dick heard it too, and faced round with a quick flush.

It was just at this moment that Peter Blyth came into the room, standing just inside the doorway. He saw instantly that something was afoot, and said to the servant at the door:

'Who is that, Stephens? that gentleman with the shiny hair, with his back towards us?'

'That, sir? I think his name is Mr Measly Shostoo, or words to that effek!'

'Mr how much?'

'Measly Shostoo, sir. I didn't hear him pernounce it hisself, for I was a-taking of the 'ats in the 'all, but only on the transgression.' Just then, Dick turned, and Peter saw him, and instantly recognized the situation. He hurried in, but too late to be of any immediate service, and stood by, ready.

Esse did not know exactly what she should do, but instinctively she put her hand up, and said with a smile:

'Oh, Dick, Dick! not before all these people! They'll think you are making game of me.' One of the smart young men here said:

'Making game of her! He is a hunter! Good!' Dick turned on him like lightning:

'Dry up there, mister! I don't make game of no female of her sex; and I don't allow no man to say I do, see? Look ye here, Little Missy, this is honest Injin, a right square game;[3] and, durn me, but

---

[3]   That is, a fair game, which in the subsequent dialogue turns out to be American draw poker.

I mean it down to my boots. This ain't no ten-cent ante, no bluff on a pair, but a dead sure thing – a straight flush, ace high!' Instantly there was a chorus of ironical remarks from the men all round:

'I straddle the blind!'

'Raise him out of his boots, pard!'

'I go you two chips better!'

'Make it a Jack-pot!'[4]

Dick looked around again scornfully, but as he did so he caught Esse's eye, and seemed to recognize the story which it told; the ripple of laughter around, however, filled up the blanks, where there were any to fill. Dick felt that he was fooled. He was, as may have been seen already, a vain man, all the more vain because of the consciousness of its own strength. Hitherto in his life he had only been tested in ways that brought out his natural force and left it triumphant; and the habit of his life was behind him to resent an affront. He glared at the ring of faces around him, and this time his look meant mischief to all who knew danger signals in a man's face. Controlling himself with an effort, he said to Esse:

'Little Missy, ye ain't a-foolin' me, air ye?'

'Oh, no, Dick; no, no!'

'Then I wish I had that laughin' jackass that kem all the way up

---

[4]   The preceding dialogue touches on each stage of play in the game of draw poker. According to *Foster's Complete Hoyle* (1963), after five cards have been dealt to each player and before any player looks at his or her cards, the player to the dealer's left begins the 'pot' – the sum of money or counters ('chips') to be won at the end of the game – by putting down a small sum called the 'blind.' The next player to the left may then put down double that sum – that is, may 'straddle the blind' – and this process may continue once around the table until a player chooses not to straddle the previous player's blind. Each player then looks at his or her cards and either puts down a sum called the 'ante' or drops out of the game. The remaining players may then try to improve their hands by discarding some or all of their cards and drawing new ones to replace them. After the draw, betting on the hands begins. To 'bluff' is to pretend to have valuable cards so as to force other players to withdraw from the game. To 'raise' is to exceed the previous player's bet. When two or more players remain in the game and they agree to stop with equal bets, their cards are exposed and valued. A 'pair,' two like-numbered cards, has the lowest value; a 'straight flush,' five cards of the same suit in numerical order, usually is given the highest value. Dick's 'straight flush, ace high' (also called a royal flush) tops everything else since a combination with higher-ranking cards in the sequence 2-10, jack, queen, king, ace always wins over the same kind of combination with lower-ranking cards. Players may agree before a game to halt it at the 'ante' stage if at that point no player holds at least the value of a pair of jacks and to leave the blind, straddle (if any), and ante in the pot as a 'Jack-pot' with which to begin the next game.

on Shasta to fool me – to fool me in face of all these –' Here he looked around again, and, as he did so, whipped from the collar of his coat his great bowie knife and, pressing the spring, threw it open with a dexterous jerk. No woman screamed; it takes more than a generation of ignorance of such matters to make women fear cold steel. But there was more than one woman present who in earlier days had seen just such quiet anger flame out and end in murder, and with one accord they drew back and left the men in front. Dick, seeing only men's faces, finished his scornful sentence: 'These – these swine! There he is, the laughin' jackass hisself!' he said, seeing Peter Blyth's face in the ring, where the withdrawal of the womenkind had left him in the front.

With a sudden spring he caught him by the throat with his powerful left hand, and held him as in a vice. Esse was paralyzed, and could make neither sound nor stir, and Peter Blyth found himself, for the first time in his life, face to face with sudden death. The rest of the men round feared to stir, not for themselves, for there was not one of them, being Californians, who would not cheerfully have made the battle his own; but they were all unarmed, and they feared that in his present infuriated condition Dick might do a brutal violence before he could be restrained. As for Peter his manhood stood to him. He did not flinch, but with cool, calm courage faced the situation. On one side was Dick, more dangerous than any wild animal, and ready to do anything, as he thundered out:

'Now, ye dog, tell me what ye meant by foolin' me and shamin' me this way; and beg my pardon, or by the Almighty I'll corpse ye – whar ye stand!' On the other side was Esse's quivering face, all fright; but fright of many kinds, for Peter, and for the shame of the open exposure of her secret which she saw coming. Peter Blyth did not himself quite know how matters stood: he had not yet heard of Esse's engagement to Reginald. All he knew was that Dick was there in such a rage that it might mean death and disaster and life-long sorrow to those he loved. The comedy had all at once and, with a vengeance, become a tragedy. So he was silent, and Dick, who was all man, even in his blood-madness, recognized the courage in him, and with an imperious gesture threw him off, saying:

'I suppose ye ain't no worse nor the rest. I've seen the day when

I cleared out the Holy Moses saloon in Portland for less than this. Answer me some of ye! what does it all mean?' It was a terrible situation, and in all that roomful of people, now as still as death, there was not one whose heart did not beat quickly, or seem to stand still at the thought of the potent, reckless, fatal force which seemed to have been let loose amongst them. In the midst of the silence Reginald Hampden stepped out, and Esse felt glad, and a new sense of relief, as she noticed his calm and gallant bearing. He moved towards Dick, and said with courtly sweetness:

'I hope I may speak here, since it is my privilege to speak for Miss Elstree! Look, sir! Look; the young lady! You are distressing her! I know you to be a brave man, and, from all I have heard her say to your honour, I am quite sure you would not willingly cause her harm or humiliate her. See, sir! you are crushing her to the dust!' as he spoke he went to Esse and stood beside her.

A quick flush seemed to leap up Dick's face from neck to forehead; his hand dropped, and with a sound in his throat between a sob and a gasp, he said:

'Little Missy, forgive me if ye can! I must have gone mad! This galoot[5] here was pretty right when he called me a brute. Let me get back to the b'ars an' the Injuns. I'm more to home with them than I am here. Be easy, Little Missy, an' ye too, all ye ladies and gentlemen; it'll be no pleasant thinkin' for me up yonder, away among the mountings, that when I kem down to 'Frisco, meanin' to do honour to a young lady that I'd give the best drop of my blood for – and she knows it – I couldn't keep my blasted hands off my weppins in the midst of a crowd of women! Durn the thing! I ain't fit to go heeled inter decent kempany! As he spoke he lifted his arm, and with a mighty downward sweep hurled down his bowie knife, so that it stuck inches deep into the oaken floor, where it quivered. Once more he turned to Esse:

'Forgive me, Little Missy; an' if ye kin forget me, an' the shame I've brought upon ye and yer house!' He bowed and was moving away, when again Reginald, to whom Esse had whispered, strode forward.

---

[5]   'Galoot' is a US term designating an awkward, strange, or uncouth fellow but also sometimes connotes affection as well.

'No, sir! You must not go like that. There is a mistake here which must be set right! You will understand me when I tell you that Miss Elstree has done me the honour to consent to be my wife. You have been put in a false position. It is quite true that Esse wished to see you; that she asked her friend, Mr Blyth, to carry such a message to you. Believe me, that she does understand and appreciate the honour that you have done her, though, I must say, in some justification of these other ladies and gentlemen, in so unconventional a manner. But you must not leave the house in such a way! Believe me, you are, and ever shall be, an honoured guest in a house to which you have saved so dear a life!' And he put his arm round Esse who had got suddenly pale and seemed about to faint.

'One of you boys,' he said, 'pick up Dick's knife and give it to him. I can't move yet!' One of the young men took the handle and tugged at it, but in vain. There was a laugh; another tried it, but with the same effect. A smile stole over the pale anger of Dick's face; he was beginning to yield to the humour of the situation, and he stood silent where he was. Mrs Elstree came forward, she had only just come into the room, having been in the music-room, and did not understand what was going on, but seeing Esse's head drooping had flown to her side. Reginald, finding her mother's arms round her, left her side and striding forward, seized the handle of the bowie knife. With a sharp jerk, and with a force which made his arm tingle from wrist to shoulder, and sent the blood up into his head, he plucked it from the floor[6] amid a buzz of

---

[6]   This action suggests that Reginald is to be thought of as a modern-day King Arthur since it parallels the incident in Arthurian legend in which young Arthur, whose identity as the son of the late King Uther Pendragon has been concealed by Merlin from everyone including Arthur, passes the test for becoming the next king by being the sole person in the realm to succeed in pulling the sword Excalibur from the large stone in which its blade has been embedded. For the classic source of this story in English, see Chapters 4-9 of Sir Thomas Malory's fifteenth-century romance, *Le Morte Darthur*. Arthur was a familiar part of late Victorian cultural knowledge, and Bram Stoker must have been reminded of the Arthurian legend and probably of the *Morte* and the sword-in-the-stone incident when, according to biographies of his employer Henry Irving by Austin Brereton (1908) and Laurence Irving (1951), in 1892 or 1893 Irving asked J Comyns Carr to write a drama about Arthur. Carr published his *King Arthur* in 1893 and claimed that it was based on the *Morte*; Irving staged it in January 1895. The play's prologue, though, is based on Malory's Book I, Chapter 25, which – in contradiction to the earlier chapters – has Arthur receive Excalibur from a hand which rises mysteriously from a lake.

approval, and a responsive 'Good!' from Dick as he slapped his thigh in his old fashion. He stepped over to Dick, shutting the knife with an experienced jerk, and held it out him: 'Your weapon, sir!' he said, 'but I should be very proud if you will let me keep it, in memory of a brave man to whom I and others owe so much!'

'Take it,' said Dick, 'an' welkim! The poor thing 'll never, I am sure, be disgraced by ye as it was to-night by me. Shake! Ye're a man, ye are; and I wish you and Little Missy all the happiness in the world!'

The two men shook hands and Reginald went on:

'You'll let me give you this in exchange, I hope.' He drew from his pocket, and detached from its gold chain, a beautiful hunting knife. 'It is not merely that it is mine, but it was given me by an emperor, who was good enough to say I had done him some service when a wild boar charged him in a Thuringian forest.'[7] Dick took the knife:

'I'll take it and keep it, pard, because on my soul I believe it will pleasure ye if I wear it! An' now, good night, an' I humbly ask all

---

[7]   Thuringia is an area in central Germany noted for its mountainous Thuringian *Wald* or 'Forest.' The European wild boar stands as much as three feet high, has sharp tusks, and has been a favourite quarry for hunters because of its strength, speed, and ferocity. In the 1880s and early 1890s all three European emperors – Francis Joseph (1830-1916) of Austria, William II (1859-1941) of Germany, and Alexander III (1845-1894) of Russia – were avid hunters, although Francis Joseph was probably the most energetic, with a tally of 48,385 head of wild game killed by 1900. In an 1892 photograph of William II in a hunting party in Germany, he wears on his belt a beautiful thigh-length sheath knife with a short guard, a bright, tasseled cord, and an ornamented, slightly curved handle. Among various British and American journal articles on his hunting activities in the early 1890s, Henry Fischer's 'The Kaiser as Sportsman' in the September 1895 *Munsey's Magazine* describes his annual 'Hubertas hunt' for 'the imperial family, princes and princesses of the blood, and all the great aristocrats' in which a roe, stag, or boar is released into woods and pursued and then held at bay by dogs, whereupon the first of the mounted hunting party to reach the scene dismounts and dispatches the quarry with a knife, 'a feat that requires some skill and involves a spice of actual danger.' The inclusion of a British painter in an imperial, European hunt seems unlikely, but intermarriage between the British and other royal families did foster international social relationships, including hunting parties. The specific nature of the hunt in which Reginald plays his heroic part is not clear, but imperial hunting was a well publicized and familiar display of aristocratic manhood and privilege at the time of the publication of *The Shoulder of Shasta*. (For the emperors, see Mikhail Iroshnikov and others, *The Sunset of the Romanov Dynasty*, 1992, and Alan Palmer's *The Kaiser*, 1978, and *Twilight of the Habsburgs*, 1994.)

yer pardon for my conduct! Forget it and me if ye can!' and he moved to the door.

Here Mrs Elstree spoke out; Esse had been whispering to her during the foregoing:

'No, no, Mr Grizzly Dick, you must not go! There is no one who can come into my house that I could be more glad to see. You must stay and show us all that you forgive us that we have amongst us made you, for a time, uncomfortable!' He paused, and Esse stepped up to him, her eyes this time full of tears, and said:

'Yes, Dick, do stay; if only to show me that you forgive me! And that you are not unhappy for what has passed. Dick – D – D – Dick, sh – sh – shake!' her tears fell as he clasped her two hands and whispered to her:

'Lord love ye, Little Missy, I ain't a-goin' to be onhappy. Why, I only kem down from the mounting because I heerd tell that it was like ye wanted me. I didn't believe it myself, an' I feared it would be a mistake if ye did. But that wasn't my affair, but yourn; an' whatever ye'd do would be right enough for me. An' as to forgivin'! – Wall of course I'll stay if ye wish it. I think I've made this jamboree[8] pretty dismal enough already, without refusin' to do anything I kin do to help make it lively again.' Another voice now joined in, that of the young lady who had commenced the trouble.

'Yes, stay! Do stay, Mr Grizzly Dick, and presently you must dance with me, if only to show me that you forgive my bad manners and my unkindness of heart. And if you do tread on my toes, I guess we'll be about even!'

'Done with ye, miss; but I'm afeerd this here rig out[9] of mine ain't jest exactly the thing for a fash'nable party. So ye'll hev to excuse me.'

'Never mind, Dick,' said Reginald heartily; 'we are all friends of yours here! If there are any who are not so, then they are no friend of our hostess or of me either; and I'll stand back to back, if you'll let me, when we slice up the last of them!' Dick smiled a good ten-inch smile, and just then catching sight of Peter Blyth's face he

---

[8]   Originally, US slang for 'a noisy revel.'
[9]   Colloquial for 'costume, outfit.'

slapped his thigh and burst out into a peal of laughter. Going over
to him he held out his hand saying:

'Ye'll forgive me, pard, won't ye; though I mighty near skelped
ye? Ye took it well though! Durned, but ye took it standin' with yer
boots on! I only hope I'll take it as well when my time comes; fur ye
had a close call that time – closer'n ever ye'll hev it again. Shake!'
the two men shook hands, and Peter Blyth, within his mind's eye
the recollection of their first meeting, roared with laughing too.
Then Reginald came and slapped him on the shoulder and said:

'Come with me, Dick. I've got something that will make you feel
more comfortable than this Sacramento rig out!' Then he
straightway took him off to his own room.

Some fifteen minutes afterwards there was a buzz of admiration
through the room when Dick entered, clad in a hunter's outfit,
something like his own, which Reginald had some time before
bought from the Indians as a model for his work.

There was about him something so fresh, and wild, and free – so
noble a simplicity and manhood, that more than one woman present
did not wonder that Esse had asked him to come down to 'Frisco.[10]

THE END

---

[10] The novel seems to end abruptly in contrast to Stoker's well known *Dracula* (1897),
which concludes with a tableau representing the solidarity of the surviving major
characters – Jonathan Harker, his wife Mina, Dr Van Helsing, Dr Seward, and Lord
Godalming – and with a confirmation of the marriage between Harker and Mina by the
presence of their son Quincey, named after their American friend who died while
helping to dispatch Dracula with his bowie knife. In *The Shoulder of Shasta*, having just
exhibited its American's lack of sophistication, Stoker returns to the simple, rugged
nobility Dick has exhibited through most of the novel for its final image while allowing
the reader to recall that the tableau of major characters is present, although not
described, since it has just been preserved by the whispered instructions of Esse and that
the issue of what seemed to Peter Blyth 'an undesirable marriage' in Chapter 7 has been
resolved by the engagement between the now-mature Esse and Reginald.